THE SHERIFF

THE MEN
OF WHITE SANDY

SARAH M. ANDERSON

Dedication

To Amy Alessio. Thank you so much for being the voice of reason when I'm anything but!

Thank you Newton Love and Annette Love Hatton, as well as the Lakota Language Consortium, for all their help with the Lakota translations in the book. Many thanks to Mary Dieterich, Mel Jolly and Karen Booth for being awesome. Finally, thanks to my husband and son—the best heroes ever!

Chapter One

Tim Means knew before he even got out of his police cruiser that he'd gained a guest overnight. The lights were on in the White Sandy police station, a small building that was better suited to a strip mall in nearby Rapid City, South Dakota, than it was in the middle of nowhere on the White Sandy reservation. Yesterday had been quiet—Mondays usually were. Tim had not so much as issued a ticket.

He sighed. He'd made damn sure to lock the station up tight when he'd gone home at seven last night. And since Jack Red Deer, Tim's deputy, was currently on loan to the FBI for a missing persons case the next reservation over, no one else should have been in the building in the last ten hours.

This only meant one thing. The thorn in Tim's side, Nobody Bodine, had been dispensing his own brand of justice again.

Damned vigilante. Tim had enough trouble keeping law and order on this rez without having to contend with some self-appointed guardian angel. Even if a guardian angel was usually on the right side of the law, he gave Tim nothing but headaches.

Vigilantes could not arrest people and, when Nobody broke into the station and threw someone into

1

lockup, Tim rarely had a choice but to let them go. Unlike Nobody, Tim was familiar with the law. Miranda's rights, protections against unreasonable search and seizure—Tim worked to uphold those things and Nobody undermined him every damned turn.

His teeth gritted in anger, Tim unlocked the police station. At least that damn vigilante had started locking up after himself. Tim had a high level of security at his station—there were more than a few people who'd like to burn his station to the ground. In fact, the only person who could get in without a key on a regular basis was Nobody. Tim had locks on the doors, bars on the windows, he'd even invested in a motion detector that would set off an alarm on his cell phone. Nobody always got around them. It drove Tim nuts.

He disarmed the sensor and called out, "Well, who do we have here?" And then he stopped.

The person in the cell was not a dead-drunk man or woman, and it was not someone who looked like they'd had the holy hell beaten out of them. Which was another one of Nobody's inappropriate "techniques."

Instead, Tim found himself looking into the wide eyes of a seventeen-year-old boy. A boy he knew too well. "Georgey? What the hell?"

Georgey sat on the floor of his cell, his knees pulled up to his chest. He had dark circles under his eyes and Tim didn't think he'd slept at all. But then, if Nobody had thrown Georgey in here in the middle of the night, well, Tim couldn't blame the boy for looking terrified. A lot of people on this rez still thought Nobody was a *sica*, a ghost. He could blend in with the shadows and remain completely unseen until he popped up and beat the shit out of you. He scared a lot of people on this rez, but he didn't scare Tim.

Georgey, however, was another matter entirely. He didn't answer, but Tim swore the boy sighed in relief that it was Tim and not someone else. Georgey closed his eyes and turned his head away, refusing to acknowledge Tim.

In a normal police station, like in a sitcom, Tim would make some calls. He would call Nobody and ask why the hell he'd dragged the seventeen-year-old boy to jail. He would call Georgey's parents and tell them to come get their kid. He would even call social services and set up a meeting. This was not the first time Georgey had been a guest of the White Sandy police.

But this was the rez. There wasn't a whole hell of a lot that was normal here. "I'm only going to ask you one more time—why are you here?"

Georgey seemed to shrink into himself but he didn't answer.

Tim shook his head. Georgey wasn't a bad kid— Tim knew what a bad kid looked like and how they'd wind up. But Georgey was wild and he had no one to rein him in. His father had been a larger-than-life man himself, loud and wild in love with the world, even if the world didn't always love him back. He'd been killed in a fight outside a bar about—well, it had to be coming up on ten years ago. And Georgey's mom? She was too drunk most of the time to give a damn what her son was doing.

For better or for worse—and today, it was worse—Georgey was basically on his own. And he had a nasty habit of picking the wrong friends.

3

Tim did not move to his desk and he did not pick up his phone. Instead, he turned on his heel and walked right back out of the police station. "Well? Are you going to explain yourself?" he said in a louder than normal voice. He didn't know where, exactly, but Nobody was close by. At least, he'd better be.

He didn't have to wait long. Even though the sun was making its daily struggle over the Black Hills, deep shadows hid the side of the station. Tim had lost the ability to be surprised when Nobody Bodine seemed to materialize out of nothing less than five feet away from him.

The man was hard to look at, but Tim could *not* be intimidated. He'd arrested Nobody enough to know that the man was real and solid and human. Scary, but completely human.

"He was alone," Nobody said.

Tim sighed heavily. All the other times he'd encountered Georgey, the boy had been part of a group. Which was a polite way of saying *gang*. The boy was so desperate for approval that he would look for it any place he could find it, and there were some men on this rez who were happy to exploit that.

Tim had cut Georgey slack before because he really was just a kid. But he was seventeen now, on the verge of becoming a man. "What was he doing?"

The light around Nobody seemed to bend, and Tim felt an electric charge raise the hairs on the back of his arms. God, if he could just get through a day without having to deal with Nobody Bodine, his life would be so much better.

"Breaking into the Clinic," Nobody said.

Tim swore and scuffed his heel against the small

wooden porch he'd built under the front of the station on his own time and his own dime. "Was he after drugs?"

Nobody shrugged. He didn't say anything—which was par for the course.

That meant Nobody had grabbed the kid before he could do anything deeply incriminating. "I can't hold him, you know. I can't keep the people you bring in. If you'd called me instead, I could've arrested him properly."

Nobody nodded. "He needs to be scared," he added, stepping back into the shadows a little deeper.

Tim stared at the man as best he could. "Are you serious?"

He thought Nobody nodded again, but the man was almost *not* there so it was hard to tell. And then he was gone.

Well, hell. Nobody was not a big fan of being locked up. He was a convicted killer who had done time. He firmly believed that only bad people belonged in jail, and there were plenty of those to go around. Nobody had appointed himself something of a guardian angel for many of the kids on this rez—kids who needed help and weren't going to get it anyplace else. Tim was one half of a two-man force and there were only so many hours in the day. Yeah, it was a pain in his ass when Nobody beat up a drunk who was beating up a kid. But even Tim had to admit sometimes, Nobody was the last line of defense for the people who needed it the most.

Like Georgey. Tim couldn't believe Nobody was actually suggesting Georgey needed to be scared straight, but the kid needed something. For too long, Tim, Jack and Nobody had been finding Georgey at the scenes of other crimes—vandalizing the Child

Care Center or the school, or on the edge of a brawl at the basketball courts.

But he'd never actually done anything on his own. He was a follower, not a leader. The problem was that he was a follower *without* a leader.

Shit. This felt big—like Tim was standing on the edge of a cliff with Georgey beside him and staring down at the nothingness below. One wrong move by either of them and Georgey was going to step right into the void and Tim would never get him back. Instead, he'd spend the rest of his days busting Georgey for petty crimes that escalated into more serious crimes. Georgey would do time and with each conviction, the sentences would get longer.

He was going to lose this kid. Already the loss felt palpable. They had so few kids left. Tim had cleaned up more suicides and overdoses over the last twelve years he'd been the law on this rez than he'd ever thought he'd see. And those who got out—the ones who got into college and left the rez? They rarely came back and, more often than not, they married outside the tribe.

Tim was not one of those tribal members who was convinced that all they needed to do to make things right again was to get rid of the white man and declare the Lakota territory a country independent from the United States. He was a realist and he knew that was never going to happen.

But he worried about his people and he worried about his place among them. He worried about kids like Georgey—all the ones who had already slipped away and all the others who were edging up closer to the cliff.

As much as he hated to admit it, maybe Nobody was right. Maybe Georgey needed to feel the fear of God.

Tim turned around and went back into the police station. He saw now that Nobody had not just tossed the kid into the cell like he did with the violent drunks. A cup and plate that held what looked like Pop Tarts sat close to the bars. Georgey hadn't touched them, but Tim was forced to admit it qualified as a thoughtful gesture. And there was a book on the bed next to Georgey—an old Western by Louis L'Amour. As crazy as it was, he knew that was Nobody trying to reach out to the kid.

Tim stood outside the cell and stared down at the ball of scared teenager on the floor. "Do you know where your mom is?"

Georgey didn't look up, but he shook his head no.

Hell. Eileen Crow Dog wouldn't come home until she was damned good and ready, and no one—not even Georgey—knew went that would be.

Tim worked hard to keep his frustration out of his voice. "What about your grandma?" Not that Darlene Crow Dog could keep Georgey under control. But she could at least come pick him up.

"She's sick," Georgey said in a voice more fitting for a ten-year-old than a teenager.

"Is there anyone else who can come get you?"

Georgey shrugged.

"We can't keep doing this, Georgey. What am I supposed to do here? Keep you locked up and throw away the key?" He saw the kid shudder. "Why were you breaking into the Clinic? And don't try to deny it. Nobody Bodine is many things but he never lies." As far as Tim knew, anyway.

7

"I told you," Georgey said in an accusing voice as his head snapped up. He glared at Tim. "Grandma is sick."

Tim stared down at the young man. "Then why didn't you call someone? Dr. Mitchell or even Rebel? They'd both have come, if she's really sick. You don't have to steal." He exhaled. "Unless you're lying." Always a possibility. People would say anything—*do* anything—when their backs were against the wall. Tim knew that only too well.

When Georgey didn't respond, Tim went on. "Who were you stealing the drugs for? Yourself? Or Dwayne LaRoche?" LaRoche—the self-styled leader of the Killerz gang—was still in jail, but that didn't mean he was out of the game.

Georgey dropped his head back to his knees. The conversation was over.

Normally this was the point where Tim would have to let Georgey go. He should, really. But, in addition to being young, Georgey wasn't exactly up-to-date on his legal rights. "Well, you can just sit there until you decide to tell me the truth," Tim bluffed. "I'm going to make some calls."

Georgey groaned but at least he had the decency to do it quietly.

Tim went to his phone and started dialing. It was early enough that Dr. Madeline Mitchell, the doctor of the White Sandy Clinic, and her husband, Rebel Runs Fast, the medicine man, were still both probably at home. He dialed the house.

"Good morning, Tim," Rebel said with a yawn before Tim had even announced himself. "How's your prisoner?"

8

That was the thing about Rebel Runs Fast. He knew things he shouldn't know and Tim could never figure if it was just because gossip on this rez ran through Rebel or if it was because Rebel was prone to visions. Tim wasn't sure how much stock to put in Rebel's visions. Those were the old ways, and times had changed.

Then again, Tim had a conversation with the moving shadow this morning, so he couldn't discount anything.

"Someone caught him trying to break into the Clinic," Tim said—although if Rebel knew Georgey was here, he probably also knew why. Rebel was one of the few people Nobody Bodine actually talked to. "He says he was trying to steal medicine for his grandma. You think you could go check on Darlene Crow Dog for me today?"

"Sure, not a problem." There was a pause, but Tim just waited. If Rebel was thinking or having a vision, Tim didn't want to interrupt. Finally, Rebel said, "This is different for Georgey, isn't it?"

Tim glanced over at the boy in the cell. It hurt him to leave the kid in there but he didn't have a choice right now. He was the law around here—not Nobody Bodine, not Rebel Runs Fast—*him*. And if he started making exceptions, people would plow him into the grass. "If you wouldn't mind having your wife make sure there was no damage done to the building?" he asked without answering Rebel's question.

There was a pause. "Are you still holding him?"

"Can you give me a good reason why I shouldn't be?"

Rebel whistled. "I thought when Nobody played the bad cop, you played the good cop."

9

Tim gritted his teeth. "You're confusing me with Jack. He's the good cop. I'm the asshole and I'll hold this kid as long as I need to."

He waited for Rebel to call him on it—he really didn't have just cause to hold the boy and, at this point, he had nothing to charge him with either. He knew damned well Nobody would never testify in a court of law, so this whole situation boiled down to he said vs. he said, especially if Nobody had gotten to Georgey before he did any damage to the clinic.

But Rebel didn't say anything. Instead, he said, "I'll check on Darlene and let you know what I find out."

"And Rebel?"

"Yeah?"

"If she can't take him, I need to find someone who can." Tim hated calling social services on kids— especially kids Georgey's age. But the kid was still technically a minor and Tim couldn't have him running wild on the rez.

"Got it." Rebel hung up.

Tim turned his attention back to Georgey, who had heard every word, no doubt. "Anything you want to tell me? Because I'm going to find out, sooner or later."

Georgey looked up and Tim could see the boy trying so hard to be tough. He didn't make it, though. The fear in his eyes shone way too bright for that. "How long do I have to stay in here?"

Tim notched an eyebrow at him. "Until I decide to let you out. Welcome to doing time, kid. If you're not careful, this is the rest of your life." He tilted his chin at the plate. "Eat your breakfast. You're not getting anything else until lunch."

Something mean passed over Georgey's face. "I hate you. You and that freak and Rebel—I hate you all."

Tim stood slowly. He didn't have the build of Nobody Bodine but that didn't make him any less formidable. He went to stand in front of Georgey's cell and stared down at him. Georgey's bravado failed him and he shrank back, as if he thought Tim would hit him.

But he didn't say anything. He didn't threaten or cajole and he didn't try to warn the kid off from the path that he was hell-bent on taking. "You don't have to like me, kid. No skin off my nose one way or the other. But I haven't given up on you yet."

Then he went back to his desk and got started on the morning's reports.

Chapter Two

Summer Collins was wincing her way through yet another terrible essay on *Romeo and Juliet* when her phone buzzed with an unfamiliar number. She didn't recognize the area code—it wasn't the Twin Cities. So she ignored the call and kept her attention focused on her students' final papers. At this point in the school year, if she never read Shakespeare again, it'd be too soon. His entire works could all be dropped into a Dumpster and she would do a little jig of joy.

"*Romeo and Juliet* is the story of a boy and a girl," Michael's paper started out.

Summer dropped her head in her hands and groaned. Clearly her plan for peer-reviewing each essay hadn't worked this year. After nine months of trying to beat literature and culture into his skull, *that* was the best he could come up with?

Was this what she'd signed up for? Was this how she was supposed to be "making a difference"? By trying to make the words of a long-dead white guy relevant to today's inner-city kids?

Her phone buzzed again. Whoever called had left a message. That was odd. Who the heck called and left messages these days—besides her mother, that was?

Summer decided to take her chances with the

random wrong number. The final papers weren't going anywhere. She called up her voicemail, expecting to hear something in Spanish or a robo-call.

"Hello," said a deep voice with a heavy accent that sounded like...home. That was the first thing Summer thought of. *Home.* "This is Sheriff Tim Means of the White Sandy police force. I'm trying to get ahold of Summer Collins or her mother, Linda. This is in regard to Georgey Crow Dog."

Summer's heart began to pound. She knew that accent—of course she did. That was the same accent her father had spoken with. Sure, she hadn't talked with him in almost fifteen years, but it was the sort of thing a person never really forgot.

"If you could please return my call at your earliest convenience, I'd appreciate it. Again, this is Sheriff Tim Means of the White Sandy police force..." He listed his number and then the call ended.

Georgey.

Her brother.

Panic flooded her system. Was the boy okay? Why were the police trying to call her? Was he dead or just in trouble?

Oh, God—her mother was going to have a fit of epic proportions about this. Summer hadn't talked to her father in fifteen years for a reason.

Her hands shaking, she hit the call back button on her phone and waited. "White Sandy Police, this is Tim. Is this an emergency?"

"Um, hello. My name is Summer Collins and I think you just called me? Is Georgey okay?"

"Ms. Collins, hello. I see you got my message."

If Summer could have glared at him through her

13

phone, she would have. He hadn't answered her question and whoever this Sheriff Tim Means was, she could throttle him right now. "Yes. You called about Georgey?"

"Ms. Collins, do I have the correct information on you? Are you related to Georgey Crow Dog?"

"Yes," she said, more frustrated by the second. "He's my half-brother. Is he okay?" she demanded.

There was a pause. Finally, the sheriff said, "Well, that depends on your definition of 'okay.' I've got Georgey in lockup right now. He tried to break into the medical clinic and steal drugs last night."

"That's not true!" Summer heard a voice shout in the background. It didn't sound like the little brother she remembered—the voice was deeper. And angrier.

"This is not the first time Georgey has been a guest of the White Sandy," the sheriff went on, as if Georgey hadn't interrupted him. "At this time, his mother is unable and unwilling to pick him up. His grandmother has been transported to the hospital in Rapid City and is also unable to get him."

"Oh." Summer didn't know how she was supposed to feel about that. She'd only met Georgey's mom once, the last time Summer's mom had taken her home to the reservation. The last time she'd seen her father. "What about Dad? I mean, what about Leonard?"

The sheriff did not reply. In the background, Summer could hear Georgey asking, "What's she saying?"

"Ma'am," the sheriff said in a gentle voice, "I thought you knew. Leonard Two Elks has been dead for almost ten years."

An odd sort of silence filled her head. It wasn't surprise—at least, not much of one, anyway. Hadn't her mother been saying, "He's probably dead, so just forget about him," for years?

No, she couldn't be surprised by this. And on some level, it almost made her feel better. It wasn't that her father had forgotten about her. He'd just…died. And she hadn't known.

"I'm…" She swallowed against a lump that had formed in her throat. "I'm sorry to hear that." What was she supposed to say? She didn't know. She didn't have a clue.

"Yes. Well, you can see the problem. Georgey," he added, as if she'd forgotten about the brother she barely knew. "I'd like to release him into the care of a guardian. But I need a guardian who will actually take care of him."

"Me?" It came out more of a squeak than a statement, but seriously?

"I take care of myself!" came the shout from the background. "I don't need anyone."

"If a blood relative can't take him," Sheriff Means said in that sympathetic voice that was beginning to drive her nuts, "then I'll have to turn him over to social services. I'm going to level with you, Ms. Collins. If he gets arrested again, I can't promise he won't do time. He's got quite a rap sheet of petty crimes and he's dropped out of school. He's on a fast train to nowhere. You may be his last chance."

"A rap sheet?" She tried to make that information fit with her last memory of her brother. The last time she had been on the White Sandy reservation. The last time she'd seen that part of her family.

Georgey had been no more than three, a fat-cheeked toddler that went too fast. He got into everything, a tiny tornado of energy that spun and spun until he dropped from exhaustion. One of Summer's jobs had been keeping an eye on him during the big pow wow. She'd been twelve and nervous about visiting the Indians. She hadn't thought of herself as an Indian before that—according to her mother, she wasn't.

During the trip, Summer played with her little brother and listened to her dad tell stories of his time in the Army and met her grandparents and Georgey's grandparents and it had all been... Wonderful. One of those warm summer memories that was hazy around the edges and perfect in every way.

And now that happy little boy was in jail for trying to steal drugs from a medical clinic. And Summer was his last hope.

"I... I can't. I mean, I'm a teacher and school's not done for the summer yet." The silence in her head transformed into something else, a little buzz that began to build. It was the sound of panic. "What are you going to do with him if I can't..." Because honestly? She had no idea what she was even supposed to do in this situation.

Bring the kid to Minneapolis to live with her? Become a parent to her brother? She was doing okay, although she had a hell of a lot of student loans to pay off and, on her teacher's salary, it was going to be a long time before she ever got to the end of that mountain. But to suddenly be responsible for another person? One who'd been in trouble with the law?

Was she seriously supposed to consider bringing

a juvenile delinquent into her apartment and hope for the best?

And that didn't even scratch the surface of dealing with her mother. If Summer brought Georgey home with her, Linda Collins might finally lose what was left of her mind. No, Summer was under no delusions about that—Linda would make Georgey's life a living hell. She'd make *everyone's* life a living hell.

"What about after school gets out?" Sheriff Means' voice was maddeningly calm. Her entire world had just shifted to a different axis and apparently his was going to keep on turning. "Could you come see to your brother then?"

"She's not my sister," Georgey shouted in the background. "I don't have a sister. I don't have anyone."

"We are all family," she heard the sheriff say—although his voice was quieter, as if he'd pulled the phone away from his mouth. It was the first time he'd responded to Georgey during the call. Then he spoke in the phone—louder than necessary. "If he can't make bail, I guess I'll have to leave him locked up."

"I hate you!" Georgey screamed.

It sounded like the kid was being tortured—which didn't entirely fit with the image she'd developed of Sheriff Tim Means. She was picturing an older man, with a beer gut that hung over his belt buckle, and graying hair. In her mind, there was a box of donuts on his desk. But that was an unfair assumption and she knew it.

She'd made plans for her break. She was going to teach summer school for extra cash and she was going to go camping and see movies and find a boyfriend—a summer fling, just for fun.

But she couldn't leave her little brother in lockup—even if he wasn't the little brother she remembered. "I can't get out there for another week and a half. But I don't want you to leave him in a cell for that long. That's not the right thing to do."

"We might have to respectfully disagree on that, Ms. Collins. It might do him good to see what's waiting for him if he can't straighten up and fly right."

The buzz in her head was now a dull roar. "Isn't there anything you can do?"

"I don't know if you noticed, but Georgey and I aren't exactly good friends." She might have been mistaken, but it almost sounded like he was laughing.

"Asshole!" came Georgey's bitter reply.

"I might have picked up on a little tension," she conceded.

"I'll see what I can arrange," the sheriff said. "He broke a window before he got caught, so I think community service is a good place to start—if that's okay with you? I can find things to keep him busy."

"Will you leave him locked up? I mean, at night?" Because community service was great but even the toughest kids might crack alone at night in jail. Or, worse, not alone.

There was a long pause. "I've got a few alternatives. I'll see what I can do."

That had an ominous sound to it, but community service was better than jail time. Probably. Almost definitely.

She'd have to completely throw her plans out the window and her principal was not going to be happy that she was going to bail on summer school, but it couldn't be helped. Georgey was family, after all. And she couldn't help but think back to when she met him all those years ago and her father had said, "Keep an eye on your baby brother, okay?"

And Summer had promised she would.

"That's fine," she said, as if she knew what she was talking about. "I'll leave for the reservation as soon as I turn my grades in. Please keep an eye on him."

"I will," the sheriff promised. "I look forward to meeting you, Ms. Collins."

Her father was dead and her brother was in jail and, for the first time in fifteen years, she was going to South Dakota.

What on earth was she going to tell her mother?

***

Tim hung up the phone and stared at it for a moment. He wasn't sure what he'd expected. Rebel had managed to talk to Darlene, Georgey's grandmother, enough to know that Georgey had a half-sister who lived in Minneapolis named Summer. Leonard's daughter. Tim thought maybe somewhere deep in the back of his mind, he knew Leonard had had another kid—but he had no memory of having ever seen or met her.

Her voice had been soft and quiet—and, yes, more than a little panic-stricken. He couldn't blame her for that. She hadn't even known her father was dead.

"Well?" Some of Georgey's bravado had faded and he sounded nervous again.

Tim was tempted to ignore the boy, but he couldn't do that for long. Summer Collins had been right about one thing—he couldn't keep this kid locked up for a week and a half. The boy may need to be scared, but that didn't mean he needed to be tortured.

Tim swung around in his office chair. "Well, what?"

Georgey stared at him. At least he'd gotten up off the floor and was now perched on the edge of the lumpy mattress. "Well, what did she say?"

"Gosh, it was awfully hard to tell, what with all the shouting." Tim notched an eyebrow at the kid. "She might have said to leave you here until you learn your lesson, but I can't be sure."

Georgey's eyes went wide as he unfurled from the bed. "What? But...but...I'm just a kid! You can't keep me locked up in here!" His face paled. "Can you?"

Dammit. Tim had a reservation to protect. He couldn't spend all his time babysitting a sticky-fingered seventeen-year-old boy. But he also couldn't just show the kid the door and say, "stay out of trouble."

Tim stood and walked over to the cell door. "You've got two choices, kid. You can stay here for the next week and a half as a guest of the White Sandy police force. You get three meals a day and some of the finest industrial-strength soap known to mankind."

Georgey eyed him warily. He looked like a rabbit surrounded by a pack of wolves—except it was just Tim. "Am I going to like the second option any better? Because that option sucks."

Tim was going to regret this. His only consolation was he was going to regret it no matter what Georgey picked. "I let you out and you do what I tell you."

"Any chance for a third option?"

Tim laughed—a genuine laugh. The kid had spirit, he had to give him that. "Nope. The station needs to be cleaned and I understand that there's a window at the clinic that needs to be replaced. I'm sure Dr. Mitchell has some other things that she needs done too. You spend a week and a half fixing the mess you made and she might not press charges. And if she does, I'll speak to the judge about your good behavior."

"You want me to clean this dump?" Georgey looked around. "This place is disgusting."

"You don't have to. You can stay locked up with all the filth. Trust me, this place is paradise compared to prison. The rats here aren't even that big. They're more cuddly than anything."

He was teasing, of course—the station didn't have rats.

Georgey didn't realize that. "You can let me out now."

Tim didn't make a move toward his keys. "There are conditions. I'm not lying when I say you have to do what I tell you. This place better shine like the top of the Chrysler building—and the Clinic, too— because if I have to put you back in the cell, you won't get out until Summer Collins arrives, and maybe not even then. And, just in case you're thinking about slipping off into the night, let me remind you that I'm not the only one who can put you back here."

At the reference to Nobody, Georgey got very serious. "Do I have to sleep here?"

"No." Tim rubbed the side of his jaw with his thumb. He didn't want to leave the kid here alone at night and he didn't want to spend the next week and a half dozing in his office chair. He'd done that before and had no desire to repeat the experience. If Jack were back, that'd be a different story. But as it stood, Tim didn't have anyone else he would trust inside the building and he didn't trust that Nobody wouldn't come in anyway and scare the kid some more. "You're going to come home with me."

All the blood drained out of Georgey's face. "What?"

"Your choice, kid. You can stay in the cell or you can sleep on my couch. Which is it going to be?"

Georgey slumped back on the mattress and for a second, Tim thought he was going choose the lockup. But then he sighed heavily and got to his feet. Tim hadn't realized the kid had grown another two or three inches since their last run-in. His pants didn't have a shot in hell of covering his ankles and everything about him looked…shabby and thin. Had Darlene been feeding the boy enough? How long had she been sick, with only Georgey to rely on?

"Is she going to take me away from this place?" Georgey asked in a low voice and Tim had no idea what the kid was hoping to hear.

"I don't know." He dug out his keys and unlocked the cell.

Georgey walked to the door, but he didn't step out. "What did she sound like? Did she sound…" He dropped his gaze, embarrassed. "Nice? Or… I don't want to go with her if she's like Mom."

Tim thought back to the way Summer had found

a little bit of humor in a hard conversation. Her voice had been soft and sweet and he didn't know how old she was, but he found himself hoping she wasn't...

Wasn't what? Married? *Get serious, Means*, he scolded himself. The woman was returning to the reservation under less than ideal circumstances. He didn't have the time to indulge in any little fantasies— even if they were about a woman he'd never arrested, a woman who might not look at him as if he were the scum of the earth for upholding the law.

Like too many people here did.

Besides, she was a city girl. The White Sandy was a hell of a long way from Minneapolis and she hadn't even known her dad had passed on. No, she wouldn't be the slightest bit interested in him.

Still... "She's a teacher. She sounded sweet, not mean. Not drunk."

Nodding, Georgey took the last step out of the cell. Tim swung the metal bars shut behind him. When the lock clicked, Georgey jumped. There was that fear of God, hovering just below the surface. No Lakota wanted to be locked up. Tim knew that as well as anyone. "Now what?"

"Now," Tim said with a smile, putting his arm around the boy's shoulder and swinging him toward the broom closet, "you get to experience the joy of manual labor. Do a good job and I won't make you eat prison food for dinner."

Georgey's shoulders sagged and Tim felt a little bit sorry for the kid. "Cheer up. In a week and a half, Summer Collins will be here."

Maybe her arrival was something they all could look forward to.

Chapter Three

It took a day to get from her apartment to the White Sandy reservation. A long, boring, *painful* day of driving. The farmlands of western Minnesota and eastern South Dakota were vast, all right. And none of it helped Summer's mood.

She'd had an epic fight with her mother about Georgey Crow Dog. Summer had always known that her mother was bitter about her father leaving. But the rage Linda Collins unleashed at the mere mention of Summer going back to the reservation had surprised her.

She'd always known Dad had left them. And her mother hadn't bothered to hide the fact that Dad had cheated on her while they were still married. But after last night? The things her mother had said?

Linda Collins had said—okay, screamed—so many awful things that it took most of Summer's mental energy not to remember. And the ultimatums? "You go after that bastard, you're no daughter of mine!"

Summer knew her mom hadn't meant it, not really. But that didn't mean it hurt any less. She'd already lost her father and she hadn't even known it. She didn't want to lose her mom too, because then she'd have no one.

Well, she'd have Georgey. A teenager with a rap sheet and an attitude problem.

"We are all family." Somehow, the words the sheriff had uttered—not to her, but to Georgey—were what brought her comfort now. What would it be like to have a family that stuck by you through thick and thin—even when you did something they didn't like? Her dad had bailed and her mom promised to cut her off and…

And driving through the grasslands of the Great Plains made Summer feel insignificant. Alone.

By the time the sun was blinding her, Summer had made it to the edge of the White Sandy reservation. She was tired and her butt hurt and if she never saw amber waves of grain again it'd be too damn soon. But the moment she passed the "Welcome to the White Sandy Reservation" sign, something in her chest unclenched. Fifteen years had passed since she'd been here. But it was crazy how much it felt like coming home.

Summer put the brakes on that line of thinking. This was not a homecoming. She was barely going to be here a week—two at the most. Surely she could get this whole situation with Georgey straightened out by then. His mother would be found or his grandmother would get out of the hospital or…or…or aunts and uncles, right? On his mother's side?

Or even on his father's side? Were there more relatives she didn't know she had? Her father's parents were dead, that much she knew. But there had to be someone who could take the boy, right?

What if there weren't anyone else? Then what? Would she be able to take Georgey back to Minneapolis with her? Could she afford to clothe and feed a teenager on her salary? Would Georgey stay out of trouble or would she spend the next few years bailing him out repeatedly?

Summer was in an impossible situation and she knew it. Her best hope was that someone else would be able to take the boy. She kept telling herself someone would step up to the plate. They *had* to.

She followed the directions she'd printed out because she didn't trust her phone this far in the middle of nowhere. Which didn't help her when the road ended unexpectedly. One minute she was driving along a pea-gravel-topped road. The next, a rusted-out truck sat behind a barricade that was so old, scrub brush had grown up around it.

Summer slammed on the brakes, narrowly missing the barricade. What the hell? She studied her directions. According to them, she was supposed to follow this road for another two miles. Two miles of road that clearly didn't exist.

Now what? She pulled out her phone but she'd been right—no service here. Not even roaming.

She got out of the car to look around. She highly doubted she'd recognize any landmarks—although it was possible this abandoned truck had been here for at least fifteen years.

Nope, she didn't recognize anything. Worse than that, she didn't see anyone. When was the last time she'd passed a gas station? It had to have been a good forty miles back.

Panic began to creep in at the edges. Well. Then she'd just have to drive back to that gas station and call Sheriff Means and admit she'd gotten lost. Her pride would sting but she wasn't about to wander off into the tall grass on foot. At that pow wow fifteen years ago, her dad had told her and Georgey stories of men who'd gotten lost in the grass and eaten by coyotes waiting to trick the foolish and stupid.

Just then, she thought she heard something—or saw something? Just out of the corner of her eye? She spun but there was nothing there but the grass. "Hello?" she called out nervously as she edged toward her Corolla. "Is anyone there?"

She was acutely aware she was a single female alone in a deserted stretch of nowhere with no place to hide. And she felt, almost as much as saw, someone—or something—was watching her.

Right. This was how horror movies started. Time to go.

She got into the car and backed up. Way, way up—a good half mile before she felt the road was wide enough to pull a U-turn. When she was pointed in the correct direction, she looked in her rear-view mirror and saw... *something*. Definitely something.

Summer stepped on the gas, sending a hail of gravel out behind her. So much for the reservation feeling like home. At least back in Minneapolis, dark shapes that didn't look entirely human didn't stalk you through the grass.

After a few miles—and no one chasing her car—Summer's heart began to beat at near-normal speeds again. She slowed down to reasonable speeds and looked around. Maybe if she saw a house or something? She remembered the pow wow overflowing with people in both fancy outfits and regular clothes. All those people had to live somewhere on this reservation, right?

She saw no one. And the emptiness was starting to get to her. She'd been in the car since four that morning. She was tired and grumpy and more than a little freaked out. She missed her nice apartment and her safe life and she even missed grading those awful student papers.

Just as she approached the *T* in the road, she saw the most wonderful thing ever—a cop car. Even better, it was slowing down! Dear God, please let it be someone on the White Sandy police force.

The car pulled off to the side of the road at the intersection. Summer's breath caught in her throat as she watched a man get out of the car. Was this the same man she talked to on the phone, Sheriff Means? Because the man striding toward her looked absolutely nothing like the man she'd pictured in her head.

Instead of short hair streaked with white, he had long black hair that came down just below his shoulders. It wasn't even tied back in a tail—instead, the breeze caught it and blew it around him. The man she'd pictured had a gut—too much beer and too many donuts. But the man who was now walking around her car was lean and muscled and moved with a coiled grace that did more than catch her breath—he took it away.

He stood by the driver-side door while she gaped at him. She hadn't remembered much about her brief time on the reservation, but she remembered what her father looked like. Now that she thought about it, her father and the way she'd envisioned this officer looking weren't that different. Large and heavyset with short hair going white.

He had on a nametag. *Sheriff Means*.

One corner of his mouth quirked up into an amused smile and he made a motion for her to roll down her window.

Oh, damn. She'd just been sitting there, staring at him. She quickly rolled down the window. "Sheriff Means?"

He nodded his head in acknowledgment. "Ms. Collins?"

"Yes. Call me Summer." She didn't know why she said that. She was Ms. Collins to her students. She was perfectly fine answering to her last name.

"Then you have to call me Tim," the sheriff said, his warm brown eyes doing something that looked remarkably like twinkling.

Was he laughing at her? Or flirting?

She jerked her gaze away from his face. Was it hot in here? "How did you know where I was?" She looked around at the nothingness surrounding them. "I mean, I don't even know where I am and there's no one around. Except…" She looked in the rearview mirror but she didn't see that *something* that had been there earlier.

Sheriff Means—Tim—stiffened and turned to look behind the car.

"What is it?" she asked, a bit of that panic coming back up. At least this time, she wasn't alone. She had an officer of the law—she glanced down and saw that he had a gun at his side. An *armed* officer of the law. Whatever that shadow thing had been, she wouldn't be scared anymore.

Tim was scowling at the open space behind her car. "You saw something, I take it?"

She nodded, unsure if she was supposed to feel

silly for fearing shadows or terrified that he knew what she'd seen.

"You have nothing to worry about," he went on, setting his hand on the roof of her car and leaning down closer. Tobacco—not cigarettes and not cigars but the good kind of tobacco she'd only smelled during that one pow wow—wafted around him. She leaned forward and inhaled deeply. "What you saw was an…associate of mine, if you will. He seemed to think you might get lost and so he was keeping an eye out for you. He let me know where you were."

How the hell was she supposed to interpret that statement? "It didn't look like a man," she said, feeling stupid. "It was like some sort of shadow."

Tim grimaced. "Yeah, he does that. I'll introduce you, if it'd make you feel better." He sounded hesitant about this. Summer must have given him a look, because he added, "Been a while since you've been on the rez?"

Her cheeks heated. "Is it that obvious? I haven't been here since I was twelve and so far, I've gotten lost and seen an *associate* of yours." She knew she was not putting forth the most competent of first impressions. Why would anyone trust her to make decisions about a teenager?

The lazy grin lifted the other corner of Tim's mouth. How old was he? He had that kind of ageless face that meant he could be anywhere from twenty-five to forty-five.

She remembered the reason she was here in the first place. "Where's Georgey?"

Tim shifted, his hips moving side to side and she was absolutely not staring at the fluid motion of his body. Really, *really* not. He brought his hands down. No ring. Why was she even looking? She wasn't. She was only going to be on this reservation long enough to do...something with Georgey. To make sure Georgey was well cared for.

The way Tim was grinning at her made it pretty clear she was making a fool of herself. God, she was screwing this up so badly.

"My deputy is keeping an eye on him. Don't worry—the boy isn't going anywhere."

She stared up at Tim in confusion. "You kept him locked up? You promised me you wouldn't!"

Something in his face changed—closed, almost. "I didn't lock him up," he said in a dull voice. "I know you don't know me or know how things work here, but I'm a man of honor."

Her cheeks got even warmer. Why was it so damned hot here? "I'm sorry. I didn't mean to—"

Tim gave a little shake of his head and stepped back from the car. "Follow me. I won't let you get lost." Then he turned on his heel.

As Summer watched, he opened his car door and set one foot in the vehicle, then turned and stared off into space behind her. He touched two fingers to his forehead in a small salute and Summer twisted in her seat to see if there was really a man back there. But there was nothing. Nothing but grass and more grass.

Sheriff Tim Means was right about one thing. She didn't know him and she had no idea how things here worked.

It took close to twenty minutes of following Sheriff Means before Summer saw actual, real buildings. Not burned-out shacks or rotting hulks of old trailers, but a solid, substantial building. Or what was two buildings sharing a connected wall? Cars were parked haphazardly because there wasn't a true street front, nor was there a paved parking lot. Children played off to one side of what looked like the newer of the buildings.

The cop car parked and Summer parked next to it. "Is this the police station?" she asked when she got out of the car.

"No, ma'am," Tim replied. He pulled a cowboy hat out of the car. It was black and when he settled in on his head, it gave him a more dangerous air. "This is the White Sandy Clinic. Georgey broke that window when he tried to get inside. Said he was trying to get drugs for his grandma, Darlene, and it turned out she was sick. But I don't know why he didn't just bring her down. Dr. Mitchell would've seen her, even if they couldn't afford to pay her anything."

"Do you think that's what he was doing? Trying to help his grandmother?"

Tim shrugged and she saw the ripple of muscle beneath his shirt. How could she have ever thought this man would have a donut gut?

"Hard to say." He motioned with his hand toward the front door and they begin to walk, albeit slowly. "Georgey is a follower. A couple times, he's almost been sucked into gangs. I've managed to keep him out with a little help, but it's entirely possible that he was stealing drugs on orders from one of the gang leaders."

Summer stopped in her tracks. She looked up at Tim—he was maybe three inches taller than she was and apparently all muscle. "Gangs? You have *gangs* here? I thought that was just an urban problem."

Tim stepped in close—so close that if she wanted to, she could have put her hand on his chest. Not that she would ever do anything like that, of course. She didn't even know this man.

"He almost joined the Killerz a couple years ago. Gangs run a lot of drugs here—the rez is a hard place to live and a lot of people want to escape any way they can. An associate of mine managed to put the leader of the Killerz out of commission and the feds helped me break up that ring, but another gang grew up in its place."

"Why? Why would anyone do that?" She felt dumb for asking, but she really had no idea. She'd heard about Mexican cartels in the news. She wasn't so naïve as not to realize that some of her students were members of gangs. But they were so far removed from that here. Hell, they were removed from everything here.

Tim tilted his head, as if he were deciding what he wanted to tell her. "I take it you aren't familiar with our ways?"

If she could stop blushing in front of this man, that would be awesome. "No, not really. Why?"

He settled his hands on top of his belt, near his gun. She got the feeling he was a hell of a good shot. "We are a warrior people. Even your father was a warrior. He left the rez to join the Army and, as I understand it, that's when he met your mother. Gang leaders take our proud warrior past and twist it. We used to have hunting raids and steal ponies from our enemies. We'd count coup and steal feathers. Now they run drugs and do drive-by shootings. For some people, there isn't much of a difference."

A warrior people? She'd certainly never thought of her father as a warrior. She had so few memories of him before he left them, and the man that she had met when she was twelve was nothing like a warrior. He'd been loud and drunk and doughy. She'd loved him anyway because he'd made her feel like she belonged to something she didn't get from her fair-haired mother and her German heritage. But a *warrior*?

She wanted to understand, but she didn't. "And you? Are you a warrior, too?"

Tim looked down at her, his eyes in shadow under the brim of his hat. "We all have our own battles to fight."

Before she could come up with a response to that, he turned on his heel and took long strides towards the clinic.

Summer stared after him. She didn't like this confusion. She was an intelligent person with multiple college degrees who'd made a nice life for herself. She was not an idiot.

Except none of that counted here. All her education and street smarts meant nothing on the reservation.

She hurried after Tim. As she got closer to the building, she could see a tall, thin man and a shorter, broader one. The thin man was scraping a putty knife along the edge of the window frame and the shorter one watched him while talking to a beautiful young lady in medical scrubs through the empty window frame.

Summer was immediately jealous of the other woman. Her long black hair hung straight past her butt and she had deep bronze skin and cheekbones sharp enough to cut glass. She looked Native in a way

Summer never had and never would. Most people didn't believe Summer was half Lakota because she simply didn't look like their idea of an Indian.

Tim strode up to the shorter man. "He give you any trouble, Jack?" He tilted his chin toward the thin man.

Jack snorted. "The kid knows better than to run from me."

It was the kind of ominous statement that made her wonder exactly what sort of place she'd arrived in. This Jack made it sound like he would hunt the other man down.

It was only then that the taller man made eye contact with Summer. And suddenly, she knew he wasn't a man—he was Georgey. There was something about him that she recognized instantly. It was the eyes. They were darker brown than hers but somehow, it was almost like looking into a mirror. "Georgey?"

Up close, she could see now he wasn't quite yet a man. Yes, he was tall and thin, but he was gangly in that way teenage boys were when they were in the middle of a growth spurt. He hadn't grown into his feet and hands yet. When he did, he was going to break a lot of hearts. But right now?

Right now, she recognized the same sullen teenage look so many of her students had when she made them read *Romeo and Juliet* out loud. He didn't want to be here and he didn't want to see her.

Georgey didn't say anything. He just stared at her for a minute until finally, Tim stepped over and smacked him on the shoulder. "Say hello to your sister. She drove a long way to see you."

Summer winced. One of the hard and fast rules of teaching in the Minneapolis public school system was you were not allowed to touch a child under any circumstances. Even things such as pats on the back were frowned upon.

But no one else seemed to think anything about the contact. Instead, Georgey looked sheepish. "Hi."

Summer couldn't help smiling. Okay, so she was completely clueless as to how things worked here. If there was one thing she knew, though, it was how to deal with sullen teenage boys. "Hello, George. I'm Summer Collins—do you remember me?" She was tempted to ask if he remembered her babysitting him at that the pow wow, but that was the sort of detail that tended to embarrass boys. They never liked to be reminded they had been babies once. So she held onto that for when they were in private.

Because they were not in private now. In addition to Tim and Jack and the young woman, there was a waiting room full of old, frail and very sick people who were watching them through the empty window. Additionally, a woman sitting behind a desk with bouffant hair—there was no other way to describe her curls—was staring and an absolutely huge man wearing medical scrubs who looked like he should be a mercenary, not working in a clinic, had paused to watch as well.

And behind them was—Summer blinked, but the vision didn't change as the woman walked forward. "Hello, I'm Dr. Madeline Mitchell," the white woman said. She had a mass of blond curls pulled back into a low bun. She reached through the empty space and shook Summer's hand.

"Summer Collins," Summer said, feeling a little dazed. This was very different from the pow wow she remembered. And she hadn't even gone inside the building!

"Thank you for coming," Dr. Mitchell went on as if she were in complete control of the situation—which she appeared to be. "I appreciate that Sheriff Means is making the young man repair the damage. He's doing a good job and I don't anticipate that we will be pressing charges. I do ask that you make sure he pays Sheriff Means back for the window."

Summer glanced at the sheriff, who did that little half-shrug again. "We can settle up later," Tim said. Then his gaze cut sideways. "Can't we, kid?"

Georgey glared, but the older man only grinned wider.

People were staring at her. The people in the waiting room, the huge guy in medical scrubs—even if they weren't flat-out staring, they were all watching her out of the corners of their eyes as she literally stood on the outside, looking in. Did they know who she was? Should she know who they were? Were any of them related to her?

Dr. Mitchell stepped in a little bit closer and dropped her voice. "If you have any questions, just let me know. I know what it's like to be the outsider here."

"But I'm not an..." The protestation died as Summer looked around again. She didn't fit in here just because Leonard had been her father and Georgey was her brother. One trip to the reservation did not give her bona fides.

An overwhelming sense of loss snuck up on her. Why hadn't she come back sooner? Well, she knew the answer to that—there was no way in hell her mother was going to bring her. And then she'd gotten busy with life—college, getting a job, teaching.

She turned her attention back to Dr. Mitchell. "Thanks," she said, smiling widely. "I appreciate it."

Dr. Mitchell gave a brisk nod and turned back to the clinic. "Jenna? We have patients waiting." The young woman in scrubs gave a brief nod before throwing a half-smile back at Jack.

Summer glanced over and found Georgey watching her. He hadn't answered the question, she realized—did he remember her or not?

Then she caught Tim Means watching her as well.

And that brought up a whole different set of questions.

Chapter Four

Summer Collins was not what he'd expected. Even now, watching her watch her half-brother, he couldn't stop staring at her. At her freckles. They fascinated him in a way he never would've expected. There was a resemblance between her and Georgey—more than enough to make it clear they were related. But Summer was also clearly white. Her eyes were a soft, beautiful hazel and her hair so light it was almost dark blonde. And there were those freckles, scattered across her cheeks and nose like sprinkles on an ice cream cone.

She was beautiful. He couldn't remember the last time he'd looked at a woman and seen nothing but beauty instead of a problem he needed to manage or situation he needed to contain. She looked much as she had sounded—sweet and gentle and maybe a little delicate.

"Can I go now?" Georgey said sullenly. Which described the last week and a half. Sullen.

He asked Summer, but she turned to Tim. She had a hell of a body. She was much shorter than Georgey, but they had the same lanky frame. Except on Summer, it wasn't lanky at all. Her body was lithe and slender and her jeans hugged her hips.

"Sheriff Means?"

Crap, he was staring. He turned back to the hole in the wall. "I don't see a window yet," he observed.

"This is bullshit," Georgey muttered under his breath.

Before Tim could tell the kid to watch his mouth, Summer swung back on him and suddenly she looked ferocious. "You will watch your mouth, young man. I do not tolerate that sort of language." It didn't come out harshly, but Tim felt the weight of her words.

The expression on Georgey's face was one step removed from an open snarl. "Or you'll what? Report me to the principal? You're not my mom."

Tim took a step forward, but Jack put his hand on Tim's arm to hold him back.

Summer's eyes narrowed. She jammed her hands on her hips and scowled up at Georgey, who had the good sense to look cowered. One of these days, the boy would learn to hold his tongue.

"I am your sister and your elder and you will not speak like that around me."

Not bad, Tim thought. She might just have the stuff to make this work.

"You can't tell me what to do," Georgey said. This time, Jack didn't hold Tim back.

"I can leave you here," Summer said before Tim could get to the kid and throttle him. She glanced at him and notched an eyebrow. "Sheriff Means made it clear that he has plenty of work for you."

"I sure do," Tim said as Summer launched a smile at him that did some mighty funny things to him. He wasn't used to women smiling at him. Most of the time, people were not happy to see him. Even women who were getting beat up by their drunk, abusive men weren't happy to see him. Yes, they wanted the beatings to stop, but they didn't want him to arrest their partners.

He didn't have the time to moon over a pretty lady—especially not one who was probably only going to be here for a couple of days, tops.

"Man," Georgey groaned and then he picked up the putty knife and went back to work on the window frame.

Tim shot a look back at Jack, who was grinning like a coyote. He pointedly glanced at Summer, then back at Tim, raising his eyebrows in question. Jack was a hell of a tracker but the man was a prankster through and through. Tim scowled a warning and moved over to where Summer was watching Georgey work. "Can I talk to you—privately?"

Was it his imagination, or did her eyes darken slightly as she turned her face up to his? "Sure."

They headed back toward the cars, but then Jack called out, "Awáŋič'iglaka yo." *Watch yourself with her*. Half of the waiting room started chuckling, which caused Summer to turn back and give him a questioning look.

He was going to find himself down a deputy if Jack didn't knock that shit off. "Níš-eyá taŋyáŋ awáŋič'iglaka yo, Jack," he shot back. *You watch yourself instead*. Clarence, the male nurse, snorted in amusement. A few of the older ladies gave him a smile. One older man gave him a thumbs-up.

Great. Just freaking great. Was his attraction to her that damned obvious?

"Is everything okay?" Summer asked, her eyes

wide. She gave no indication that she understood, which was for the best, all things considered.

"Fine," he said through a tight smile. "Shall we?"

If the clinic had a window, he might have talked to her there. But currently, there was nothing separating the inside from the outside, so it was pointless. Tim led the way back to where their cars were parked at the end of the lot, far away from eavesdropping ears and smart-mouthed deputies. He leaned back against the hood of his cruiser and crossed his arms. "As you can see, he's got a little bit of an attitude problem."

Summer laughed, a light sound. "I teach ninth grade English at a city high school. Attitude problems are what I deal with all day long."

Tim couldn't help but grin. From the way she'd reacted during their first phone call, he'd been afraid she wouldn't be able to handle this. But he should have known she'd be tougher than that. "So what do you want to do?" The question hung in the air and Tim realized what he'd said. "About Georgey, I mean."

Stupid, stupid, *stupid.*

He tried again. "Where are you staying tonight?" he asked, although he already knew what the answer was going to be.

Color came into her cheeks. "I was going to try and find a hotel," she said, sounding sweet about it. "But I'm beginning to think that's not going to happen."

He didn't even try to hide his grin. When was the last time he'd grinned at anyone? His was not a happy, smiling kind of job. "The nearest hotel is about an hour and a half away, in Wall. It's not a bad drive, but it is *a* drive." He waited for a moment, but she didn't say anything else. She just looked at him with those big wide eyes of hers and he fought the urge to stroke his thumb over her freckles. "You're more than welcome to do that, but if you'd rather not…"

"I was in the car for a long time today. I'm not sure I want to spend another three hours in it every day."

Was it his imagination, or had she leaned closer?

No, dumbass. It was his imagination.

"Did you have any suggestions?" As she said it, she dropped her gaze and then looked up at him through her thick lashes.

Hell, yeah, he had some suggestions on where she could spend the night. But he had to be a responsible human, like always. "You're more than welcome to crash at my place."

Her eyes got real wide and she stiffened and he knew it had come out wrong, so he hurried to add, "I've got a nice place—and a bedroom with a door."

He wouldn't have thought it possible, but her eyes got even wider.

Could he screw this up any more? "I'll take the couch." That was what he should have said first but he wasn't in the habit of inviting women back to his place. "Georgey has been crashing on it, but it won't kill him to sleep on the floor for a couple nights. I'll put clean sheets on the bed and everything."

He didn't like feeling anxious about things. He was a decisive guy who made snap judgment calls all the time. He'd long ago learned to trust his instincts when the shit hit the fan. But this wasn't a life-or-death situation and his instincts were muddled by a pretty girl.

"Oh... Is that..." Her voice trailed off and she looked confused. Which didn't help anything.

He was talking again before he knew what he was going to say. He couldn't remember the last time he'd talked this much. "I know it may seem weird to you, but people crash all the time here. Especially during the winter, it's not uncommon to have five or six people sleeping on the floor. We're all family, after all."

She dropped her gaze to the ground and looked embarrassed. He'd said the wrong thing again.

"I don't think I belong in this family," she said in a small voice.

He didn't like it.

"I mean, I came to the reservation for a pow wow when I was twelve and that was it. Georgey doesn't remember me and why would he? I don't know anything about this place or the people here. I don't even know if I have any other living relatives—and even if I find them, I don't know what to do about them." When she looked up at him, he saw so much more than just confusion. He saw longing and loneliness and heartbreak and it cut right through him. "My own brother doesn't know me—half-brother, that is. I didn't even know my father was dead. I don't know if I belong here."

He moved. He couldn't help it. He cupped her cheek in his hand so he could lift her face and look her in the eye. "None of us can change the past," he told her. Against his will, his thumb moved over the smooth skin of her cheek, over that dusting of freckles.

She sucked in a little gasp of air as her eyes went wide again.

"But you do belong here. No matter where you go or who you are, you belong here. If you don't want to stay with me, I can find someplace else for you. Dr. Mitchell has an extra room—but she's married to the medicine man, so there might be people sleeping on the couch there, too. If you come home with me, you have a chance to get to know your brother. And he is your brother, Summer. There is no *half* about it."

"You really believe that? That we're all family?" She hadn't pulled away from him—but she hadn't leaned into his touch, either.

"I do. Time and distance don't change that." He hadn't realized his head was moving until her eyes got even wider. His face was only a few inches away from hers.

This was beyond stupid. This was sheer insanity.

He forced himself to step back. But he couldn't bring himself to apologize for almost kissing her—or touching her. So he didn't. "It's going to take a few days to sort out what to do with Georgey and I don't want to let him go until he's fixed the window."

She blinked at him then shook her head, as if she were trying to clear away a fog. He knew exactly how she felt. "Does he have anyone else? Are there any other family members that I don't know about?"

The truth was, there were a few. But she wasn't going to like the answer. "There are some of his mother's people, but most of them are in jail. And the ones that aren't shouldn't be given guardianship of a boy."

She gave him a long look. "Did you put them there? In jail?"

It almost felt like she was judging him—which

45

was how everyone else on the reservation looked at him. It helped push away any thought of kissing her. Above all else, he had a job to do. And nothing—not even a beautiful woman with freckles—could keep him from that job. "I did."

Something in her face seemed to shutter. It hurt to watch—but the hell of it was, Tim couldn't have said why. This was how people treated him, after all.

Then she looked at him again, a new resolve tightening her gaze. "I think I'd like to get to know my brother. If you don't mind..."

"Not at all." Knowing she'd be sleeping in his bed? Nope, he didn't mind a single bit. He thought back to the panicked look on her face when he'd first gotten out of his cruiser and walked up to her car. Damn that Nobody. So he added, "And my house is the safest place on this reservation. I won't let anything happen to you while you're here."

They stared at each other and Tim had that strange feeling, at least at this one thing, they were equals.

Then Summer stuck out her hand. "We have a deal?"

"That we do." He wrapped his hand around hers but he didn't exactly shake it. He just held her tight.

And then he forced himself to let her go.

Chapter Five

It was the oddest thing, knowing she was going to go home with this man and being unsure if there was anything else to his offer—the one about him letting her use his bed. While he slept on the couch and Georgey took the floor.

It felt more like a slumber party than something carnal, she thought as she filled out yet another piece of paperwork at the White Sandy police station.

But then there'd been that moment when he'd stepped into her, touched her face and leaned down like he wanted to kiss her.

That moment had been way too short. And since that moment, Tim Means had been nothing but a sheriff. He'd brought her back to the station, set a huge amount of paperwork before her and handed her pen. He'd shown her Georgey's rap sheet and filled her in on all the times he'd arrested her brother. He'd done so in a detached way that was almost clinical—which didn't mesh with the way she'd seen him treat Georgey at the clinic.

Because there, she'd seen the frustration in his face that she sometimes saw in parents' faces in meetings that usually involved the principal, the school counselor, psychologist, and a security guard or the police.

Tim Means was worried about the boy. Summer supposed that was encouraging. Georgey did have an impressive record. He was the kind of kid who was right on the edge of being written off by society.

Tim hadn't written him off yet.

However, that didn't mean she knew what to do next.

She was actively filling out paperwork to become Georgey's legal guardian and the thought absolutely terrified her. Once this paperwork went through, he would be her responsibility. Not a problem, but responsibility.

A huge responsibility.

She was going to need someplace else to live—a place that had two bedrooms and preferably two bathrooms.

She had absolutely no idea how to tell her mother she was coming home with her half-brother. It was all well and good for Tim to go on about how they were all family and she would always belong here, but that didn't change the hard fact that Linda Collins regretted marrying Leonard Two Elks. That didn't mean Linda didn't hold Georgey—and his mother—responsible for the end of her marriage.

Summer wondered if her mother regretted having her. She didn't think so, but there had been all those things she had said right before Summer left...

Summer reined her mind in and focused on the paperwork in front of her. "Do you know if he has a birth certificate or Social Security number?" she asked Tim, who was sitting at the desk opposite her. She glanced up and found him staring at her, his dark brown eyes intense and warm, like a summer day right before a storm hit. She felt caught in his gaze, unable to look away even if she wanted to.

She wasn't sure she wanted to. There was something she could almost reach out and grab hold of between them.

Tim got up and came around his desk to stand beside her. She could feel the warmth from his hip close to her shoulder—but not touching. He leaned down and started flipping through one of the files that he'd set on the desk in front of her. "I think I might have his number in here somewhere," he said, his voice low and deep. Or maybe that was just because he was so close to her now.

She remembered one of the things she planned to do this summer and couldn't because suddenly she was in charge of a seventeen-year-old boy—a summer fling. Something short and sweet and hot and very satisfying. She'd planned on going to summer concerts in Minneapolis and art gallery openings and museum talks and movies with some artistic and sensitive man by her side.

She wasn't going to get that, not now.

But the summer fling part...

"How long do you think it will take until the paperwork resolves itself?" Surely someone had to approve all this paperwork, right?

Tim stiffened next to her. "Anxious to get out of here already?" he said in a joking tone that hit Summer's ears a little funny.

"No, actually," she said, leaning toward him. He was an attractive man—okay, he was just flat-out hot. He took care of Georgey and he had come for her when she was lost, and there was that *something*

49

between them. Summer decided to grab for it. "I pretty much canceled all my summer plans. But if I'm going to be here for a while, I don't want to take advantage of your hospitality."

Tim pivoted so his hip rested against the desk as he stared down at her. He arranged his face into something that looked studiously uninterested. "What sort of plans did you cancel?"

"I was supposed to teach summer school. No one *likes* teaching summer school," she added with a grin, "but I have student loans to pay off and it was either that or get a part-time job in retail. And I *hate* retail."

He hooked his thumb in his belt loops. God, he made that look so good. "We have a pow wow in three months—if you want to stick around that long. But I understand if you can't afford to take the time off."

She shrugged. "My loans aren't going anywhere and this feels…important. I was here for a pow wow about fifteen years ago, you know? It was the last time I saw my dad and it was the only time I've been on the reservation. I feel like maybe I've missed out on something and…"

This was not the right way to ask a man if he was interested in a summer fling. She knew that. "If I'm going to be responsible for Georgey, I should understand him a little better. I mean, there are certain things all teenage boys have in common, but culturally I don't know what it means to be a Lakota." She swallowed and forced herself to look at him.

He was listening intently. "I could help you with that, if you wanted," he said. "I've lived here my whole life and I know this reservation like the back of my hand."

"Oh?" she teased. Teasing she could do. Having a sense of humor was essential to maintaining control of a classroom. "Can you describe the back of your hand?"

"It's brown," he fired back without hesitation. "And I've got a long scar on the back of my left hand." He held it out, palm down, for her to look at.

He did have an absolutely huge scar that ran the length of his hand—far bigger and meaner-looking than any accidental cut ever could look. She reached out and, after a moment's hesitation, traced her finger over the rough skin. "What happened?" She felt more than saw his body tense up. There it was again, that *something*.

Now it was his turn to shrug. "On-the-job hazard. Not a big deal."

She gaped up at him, then stared at the angry scar again. She could see where it'd been stitched closed— and there were a lot of stitches. "Are you serious?"

He shoved his hand into his pocket. "You may find this hard to believe, but most people don't like being arrested." He cleared his throat and changed the subject. "You're more than welcome to stay with me as long as you'd like. Will your boyfriend be okay with that?"

She leaned back in her chair and let the question hang for a second. If she wasn't mistaken, a certain sheriff had just fished to see if she was interested in a summer fling. Her heart began to beat a notch faster and it took everything she had to not stare at his hips. Or other parts. "I don't have a boyfriend. And you? I don't want to cause problems…"

He was absolutely still and she could imagine

51

him staking out some sort of nefarious bad guy, watching and waiting and putting himself in harm's way to protect his land.

She'd never dated a cop before. Maybe it was time.

"I'm not seeing anyone," he said in a voice that was almost soft.

"Oh, good. Then this won't be a problem?" When he didn't respond immediately, she began to panic. What if she'd misread the signals? Crap. She didn't want to make a fool out of herself. She added nervously, "I mean, if you don't mind putting up with me?"

"No," he said, something in his eyes changing—deepening. Heat began to shimmer through her body as he stared down at her. "I don't mind at all."

***

Tim unlocked the door to his house and shoved it open with his shoulder. He didn't usually bring people back to his place, so things like sticky doors and uneven floors didn't bother him normally.

But today was anything but normal.

True, he'd had Georgey sleeping on his couch for a week and a half, but the boy didn't give a damn about the finer points of home decorating. Summer Collins, however, probably did. Tim knew his house was one of the nicer ones on the reservation, but that wasn't what she was going to see. For the first time in a very long time—maybe forever—he was embarrassed by his place.

And she hadn't even gotten inside yet.

"Let me get the light," he said, walking into the dark room and heading toward the table lamp next to his recliner. He reached it without a problem—he could walk around this house blindfolded—but something made him turn back before he flipped the switch.

Summer stood in the doorway, the last dregs of daylight silhouetting her against the darkness. He couldn't see her face, just her outline, and it made her seem smaller somehow. He wanted to go to her and pull her in his arms, but then Georgey popped up behind her and Tim remembered this was not about him and her, but about that kid.

Or was it? Because there had been the conversation back at the police station where he told her to stay as long as she wanted and basically asked her to go to a pow wow with him. And that had *nothing* to do with the kid.

Tim flipped on the switch, illuminating his shabby—but clean—home. "Well, here we are. Georgey, you can sleep on either the floor or in the recliner."

Summer stepped into the room, her eyes taking in everything that was wrong with his place. The green and maroon plaid couch was threadbare and didn't match the yellow recliner. He didn't even have a coffee table, just a small side table wedged in the corner between the recliner and the couch, that held his books and the lamp. The lamp had a shade, but there were brown spots on the fabric where it'd been singed by the bulb.

The walls were an unnatural shade of light green and the floor was bare wood. He didn't even have a television—something Georgey bitched about

Sarah M. Anderson

endlessly. But when he was home, he slept. And he wasn't home that much. He basically lived at the station.

Looking around this room, it showed.

"This is nice," Summer said in a tone of voice that made it clear she was just being polite.

The hell of it was, it *was* nice. It had doors and windows and running water and electricity and a roof that didn't leak. Compared to a lot of the homes on the White Sandy, this place was a freaking palace.

But compared to what she was probably used to? Yeah, this was a dump.

Georgey cut around her, melodramatically groaning as he hefted the small bag she had packed. "Can I put this down or do I need to hold it some more?"

Tim rolled his eyes—but Summer merely shot the boy a tight smile. "Is it too heavy for you?" she asked gently. "I didn't have any problem carrying it…"

Tim bit back a snort of laughter as Georgey straightened up and stuck out his chest. Tim had to hand it to her—she had a way of subtly manipulating the boy.

Maybe this would work. He didn't necessarily want Georgey off the rez, but he wanted the boy to have a shot and Tim knew that he wouldn't get that shot here. He wouldn't get that shot living with his mother or even his grandmother, who did her best. A teenage boy needed someone more than a sick grandmother.

Summer Collins just might be the answer to Georgey's prayers. Not that Georgey knew it yet.

"Put her bag back on the bed," he told Georgey. "Then get cleaned up. You reek."

54

He'd been talking like that to Georgey for a week and a half now and it had never bothered the boy before. But unexpectedly, Georgey's cheeks shot red and too late, Tim realized he had embarrassed the kid in front of Summer. Damn.

"I'm not the only one," Georgey muttered as he trudged down the narrow hall.

Tim scowled after him then turned to apologize to Summer, only to find her laughing. "What?"

"At least he didn't say 'I know you are but what am I'," she giggled. "I'm sorry," she quickly added. "It's been a long day."

Tim did not have much to offer guests but he had the bare necessities. "You want a beer?"

Her lips parted as she exhaled gently. "Oh, that would be wonderful. Is it okay, do you think? To drink in front of Georgey?"

Tim was pretty sure he heard the kid snort from the hallway, but then the bathroom door clicked shut. "He'll probably be in there for a good thirty, forty minutes— you've got time." He walked back through the open space that was his living room, dining room and kitchen all in one and opened the small fridge. "I only have a couple of Beaumont beers—I hope that's okay?"

"That's fine."

Tim grabbed two longnecks out and popped the caps.

"So you live here all alone?"

"I know it's not much." He'd never wanted anything more—well, maybe that wasn't entirely true. But he never needed anything more before.

"If I tell you it's fine again, will you tell me it's not a third time?" As she asked the question, her gaze didn't leave his face. Then she lifted the beer bottle to her lips and took a drink. "Because we can keep doing this all night, if you want."

He grimaced. "No, I don't particularly want that." Other things, though—yeah, he might like to do a few things all night with her.

Her eyes swept around the room again and he pulled his mind out of the gutter. He wasn't making a good impression but the thing was, he didn't know how to do better.

"I have these hazy memories of my dad's place when I came to see him. It was loud and crowded—like you said, there were people sleeping on the floors. I didn't think much of it at the time, except there wasn't any television. But looking back now…" She took another drink. "I think he lived in a hovel. I remember my mom being horrified. But I thought it was fun that we had to go to the bathroom outside." Her cheeks colored prettily at this last statement. "I mean, it was like camping or something."

Tim nodded. "Yeah, that's more common here than most people realize."

Summer dropped her gaze to the bottle in her hand. "Did you know him? My father? Because I didn't. I don't know if he was a good man or a bad one. I know what my mom says about him but I don't know if that's who he really was."

He opened his mouth to respond, but just then, Georgey started singing and Summer cracked an awkward smile.

"I've got some chairs out back," he offered. "We should be able to catch the last of the sunset."

She nodded and he led the way out the back door

which, thankfully, did not require a hip check to get open. His backyard, such as it was, was nothing to write home about. He managed to keep a small square area of grass cut on the semi-regular basis and he had two old lawn chairs, plus his grill, a battered Weber. That was it.

She paused for a second before choosing the chair on the left—it was probably the cleaner of the two. Tim did not often covet the finer things in life but right now he wished he had a nice house with tasteful furniture and clean outdoor seating that a pretty woman like Summer Collins would feel comfortable in, instead of the bare-bones stuff.

"I knew Leonard," he said, picking up the previous conversation thread. "I don't know what your mom has said about him, but I know he was like everyone else who walks this earth. He was good and he was bad and most days those things were balanced but some days they weren't."

She thought on this for a while. "That was surprisingly philosophical from a sheriff."

"I've been doing this for twelve years. This can be a hard life on hard land. I've arrested friends and buried kids and..." His voice trailed off. But he couldn't bring himself to say the words.

"Yeah," she said in a way that made it clear she understood what he hadn't said.

He'd killed people. He took no pleasure in it, but he wasn't done yet and he wasn't going to let some two-bit criminal with a shotgun tell him he was.

"I suppose that's true for Georgey, too—he's both bad and good?"

It felt safer talking about Georgey than it did

57

about her father. Tim didn't want to admit how many times Leonard Two Elks had been a guest of the White Sandy police. "He's just a kid—not a bad one," he added quickly. "But he doesn't know any other way. I don't want to spend the rest of my life putting him in jail. I hate to give up on a kid."

"Me, too. Some of the kids I teach…" She sighed. "They don't have anything but the streets. They make their own families and forge identities and, like you said, you hate to give up on them. I've only had one or two students in the five years I've been teaching where I thought they really belonged in jail."

"And Georgey is not one of those kids." He turned to look at her. As the top of the sun slipped below the horizon, the colors bled out of their surroundings. He couldn't tell her eyes were hazel or her hair was a light brown. He couldn't see her freckles at all. In the dusk, she looked like she belonged here more than ever.

It was her profile, her cheekbones and her nose. Maybe she couldn't see the Lakota in her, but he could. And something he didn't understand, some whisper from deep inside his chest, told him to hold on to that. To hold on to *her*.

She turned to him. "Do you really think this will work? I mean, I know a lot about teenage boys, but my mother is not going to like this and it's going to be hard for me to provide for him on my salary alone. I'll be moving him to a big city and if he goes to school where I teach, it's a tough place."

"I've been thinking about that," Tim said, unwilling to look away from her. "About you giving up your summer job. We've got a community college

58

not too far away—Sinte Gleska. They're always trying to get teachers who can teach GED classes. I know they couldn't pay very much, but if you needed to stay for a few weeks…"

He wasn't sure why he made the offer. It was all true—Sinte Gleska really did need GED instructors because there wasn't a high school on the reservation and too many kids didn't see the value of riding a bus for a couple hours each day to go to a place where people would call them "dumb redskins" or worse.

Well, he knew why he made the offer. Because he couldn't remember the last time he sat outside drinking a beer and having a conversation with another person that didn't revolve around arrests and death. Sure, they were still talking about Georgey—but this was different.

She made it different.

She studied him. "Do you do this for all your juvenile delinquents?"

"Do what?"

"Take them in, put them to work, give up your bed for family members, find said family members short-term jobs? Is this normal for you?"

The short answer was no. But that's not what he said. "Depends on the kid, depends on the crime—but yeah, this isn't the first time I've had someone sleeping on my couch when the only other alternative was leaving them in the cell."

She didn't say anything for a long moment. She just stared at him even though he could barely make out her eyes in the deepening dark. "What did he say—Jack, your friend?"

Tim choked on his beer. "What?"

59

"At the Clinic. He said something in Lakota and you said something back and half the people laughed." She tilted her head to one side and he knew she was appraising him. "I assume it was about me. I don't know if Dr. Mitchell speaks Lakota, but I got the feeling people know better than to talk about her in front of her."

She was perceptive, he'd give her that. It shouldn't have made Tim smile, but it did. Smart and beautiful. Which had the potential to be a major problem. "Jack told me to watch myself."

He saw her head tilt toward him in the shadows. "And you replied...?"

There was a hint of edge to her voice and once again, Tim figured she was a hell of a good teacher. She talked about her rough school and her tough students but everything about her—her voice, her posture, her attitude—brooked no arguments. It might've been easy to run over a pretty young woman like her—but she wouldn't allow it.

He sighed, trying not to feel like he'd been hauled in front of the principal. "I told him he'd better watch himself instead."

"Ah," she said in a voice so soft and gentle he almost didn't hear it. She was leaning toward him and he realized almost too late that he was doing the same. The space between them was shrinking and he found himself wondering if she tasted like strawberries.

Before he got to find out, a strange current passed over the grass, like heat lightning about to strike.

Dammit. Tim stood quickly, scanning the darkness for any sign of the familiar shape. If Nobody Bodine scared the holy hell out of this woman, he and Tim were going to have a come-to-Jesus talk about it.

"What is it?" She sounded worried, but not scared. That had to count for something, he figured.

"This better be good," Tim announced into the darkness. "You're scaring my guest."

He expected Nobody to materialize out of nothing in front of him, like he always did. But that's not what happened. Instead, the man walked out of the darkness on his far right. Tim barely saw the man in his peripheral vision, but Summer must've been staring right at him when he appeared. She let out a terrified little squeak.

Tim spun toward Nobody as Summer flung herself out of her chair. Without thinking, Tim stepped in front of her, putting his body between her and Nobody. He thought about pulling his gun because he was *that* pissed that his nice, quiet evening was being interrupted. But he figured the gun would only scare Summer even more. So instead he said, "Nobody," in his most calm, rational voice—to show her there was nothing to be afraid of.

To his everlasting amusement, Nobody whipped his black hat off his head and nodded to where Summer was hiding behind Tim. "Ma'am," he said in his gravelly voice. "Good to see the sheriff found you."

Summer made that squeaking noise again and Tim wondered what he had to do to have one *freaking* day without Nobody Bodine. On the other hand, he could feel the warmth from her body against his back. He stretched one hand out behind him, hoping to reassure her that she was safe with him. She grabbed his forearm with both hands and held on tight.

"Summer, this is an associate of mine—Nobody Bodine. There's no need to be afraid." At least, there

61

better not be. Then he shot a hard look at Nobody. "*What.*"

"The Killerz are going after the Warriors," Nobody said.

Tim sighed heavily. For a few glorious minutes, he'd almost been like a regular guy—sitting in the dark, drinking a beer and having a normal conversation with a normal woman. And now those minutes were over. "Where? When?"

"The basketball courts behind the middle school."

Summer was peering over his shoulder at Nobody, as if she couldn't believe he were real and she couldn't believe Tim was talking to him. "And you're telling me this now because..."

Nobody's face was often blank and emotionless, but even in the dark Tim could see something that looked like a smile on his lips. "Because I'm not supposed to put people in jail anymore?"

Great. Just great. Of all the time for this man to take Tim's advice. "Fine. Does Jack know yet?"

"No."

Tim turned to Summer and found himself less than six inches from her. She was staring up at him with wide eyes and it bothered him that she was scared. It bothered him even more that he was going to have to leave her. "I'm sorry about this, but I have to go bust up a gang war. Will you be okay here with Georgey by yourself?"

"I...guess?" She edged out from Tim's side, but just a little. Just enough she could take a good, hard look at Nobody. "Were you the person I saw when I got lost?"

Tim glared at Nobody, who managed to look sheepish even though he was almost not there. "Yes, ma'am. Didn't mean to scare you." Which, all things considered, was a lot of talking for him. Then he turned his attention back to Tim. "I can keep an eye on the house, if you want."

Summer made that small noise again and Tim shifted so she was completely behind him again. "No, Georgey will be here with her. How many are going to be there, did you hear?" Because Tim could do a lot of damage with a shotgun but if there were going to be more than ten people, he and Jack might not be able to handle it on their own.

"All of them, I think."

Tim swore. This was all Dwayne LaRoche's fault. The Warriors had been trying to take over what was left of the Killerz for a while now. Nature abhorred a vacuum—nowhere was that truer than in the criminal underworld.

He could call for backup, but the surrounding counties weren't exactly eager to send reinforcements to the White Sandy. "You come with me," he told Nobody. If Nobody haunted the edge of the confrontation and picked off the stragglers, he could single-handedly take the fight from twenty versus two to eight or ten versus two. "But try not to kill anyone."

Summer giggled nervously behind him. But Tim wasn't joking and Nobody knew it.

"Meet you there?" Tim asked Nobody.

Nobody almost wasn't there but he nodded. Then, just before he disappeared into the darkness entirely, he paused and said, "Ma'am, my wife told me to tell you welcome to the White Sandy."

Then he was gone.

Tim needed to get a move on, but he was having

trouble getting his feet to listen. Instead, he stood there, looking down into Summer's face. "Will you be all right?" he asked again.

"Should I be scared?" She didn't sound scared. But the way her voice trickled over his skin like a cool stream on a hot summer day wasn't making what he had to do any easier.

"No," he told her. "I promised I wouldn't let anything hurt you." It was only after he finished speaking that he realized his hand had moved and he was brushing his fingertips over her cheek.

"Is that man really married?" Which, all things considered, was an interesting question. The first question most people asked was if Nobody was real.

"Yep. You remember meeting Dr. Mitchell today?" Summer's eyes got very wide. "He's married to her sister."

"Oh." She leaned into his touch and he caught her scent, a light hint of vanilla. She smelled good enough to eat. "Will you be okay? Breaking up a gang war sounds dangerous." She reached up and touched the back of his left hand, her fingers lightly tracing the scar that a drunk with a knife had left a few years back.

"I'll be fine," he promised her. More than anything, he wanted to lean down and give her a kiss—one that promised he was coming back tonight. But he didn't. He couldn't. "Stay inside and keep the doors locked," he told her. "I'll be back."

She moved before he realized what she was doing. She rose on her tiptoes and pressed her lips against his cheek. It was a sweet gesture, but it started the fire in his blood anyway.

Then she was gone. Backing away from him

before he could fold his arms round her and hold her tight. "Good luck," she said, leaning down to pick up her beer bottle.

He wanted to tell her he wouldn't be long but it wasn't in his nature to make promises he wasn't sure he could keep. He held open the door for her and watched as she settled herself in the recliner. Then he went to his bedroom. He strapped on his bulletproof vest, grabbed the ammo box and his shotgun, and strapped a knife onto his thigh. He had a feeling this was going to be messy.

Once he was loaded for bear, he stopped and poked his head into the bathroom. "Georgey."

The boy squawked in surprise. "What?"

"I have to go on a call. You're in charge of protecting your sister. If anything happens to her, you and I are going to have a little chat."

"What the hell are you talking about?" The shower curtain moved and Georgey's wet head poked out. "I'm not going to beat her up or anything. Jesus," he added in surprise as he noticed the arsenal Tim wore. "What the hell is going on?"

"The Warriors and the Killerz are going to rumble. I'm going to be busy for the rest of the night. There's a pistol under my pillow if anyone tries to get in the house. Anyone beside me, Nobody, Jack or Rebel—shoot at their feet."

Georgey's eyes got very wide. He'd been on the edge of enough rumbles he knew what was going on, but Tim hadn't told him where the firearms were in this house. "Yeah, okay."

Tim started to close the door, but then Georgey said, "Hey—Levi keeps a knife strapped to his ankle and I heard that Chuck from the Warriors keeps a handgun tucked in his waistband."

Tim opened the door a little wider. It would make sense that the boy would turn on Chuck—Georgey was most closely aligned with the Killerz. But Levi was one of his friends. "I appreciate you sharing that with me. Anything else you think I should know?" He kept his voice as neutral as he could. The kid was offering up information and Tim wasn't entirely sure why.

Georgey was still a disembodied head sticking out from the shower curtain. "You know I didn't have anything to do with this, right?"

"You've been with me for the last week and a half."

Georgey sighed. "Levi wants to take over. I don't know how far he'll go. He's been talking about getting more guns."

Tim waited. Silence was a tool. He wanted to make sure the kid had all the space he needed to finish spilling his guts.

"He might have said something about someone named Perros. Perros was gonna give The Killerz more guns." Then he seemed to realize what he was saying, because he looked afraid. "But…you won't tell him I said that, will you?"

Tim stood there in a state of shock. "Los Perros? Is that the name you heard?" This was not a good development. Tim kept his ear to the ground enough to know that Los Perros were Mexican and they were looking to carve out a bigger piece of the North American pie. *Shit*.

Georgey nodded. "Yeah—do you know him?"

"*Them*. It's a different gang." He'd been working for a long time to keep Mexican cartels from making inroads into his reservation. If the Mexicans were going to co-opt one of the local gangs, Tim's job would be that much harder. "Good work," he told the boy. "Keep this up and I might let you ride along one night."

"Really? *Cool*."

"Keep your sister safe," Tim told him as he left the bathroom. He wasn't sure why he made the offer to the boy. No one wanted a scared seventeen-year-old around when gunfire broke out. But Georgey had willingly given up some valuable information—the kind of information that could save a lot of lives in the long run. And he hadn't done it because he was in trouble or was trying to negotiate a deal.

There was hope for the boy yet.

Tim walked out into the living room and found Summer staring at nothing in particular. "I'll be back as soon as I can."

Her gaze came into focus upon him. But she didn't get up. "I'll be waiting."

"Lock the door behind me."

Tim walked out of the house and headed to work.

Chapter Six

Not much made sense at the moment. Summer still couldn't wrap her head around that man named Nobody and how he had just materialized out of nothing. Or that he was married to the doctor's sister. Or that his wife already knew Summer was here and was extending greetings.

Or that the sheriff had just walked out of his bedroom wearing enough weaponry to start a war and she had told him she'd wait up for him.

What on earth that she gotten herself into? The reservation hadn't seemed nearly this terrifying when she'd come the last time. She hadn't even been here for twelve hours and already she had been concerned for her safety at least twice.

She heard the water shut off in the bathroom. She hadn't been able to understand everything Tim said to Georgey, but she'd distinctly heard him tell the boy where his firearm was and how he was to use it to defend her. She didn't know if that was sweet or the most ridiculously stupid thing she had ever heard in her entire life. Or both.

If anyone was going to fire a gun, it was going to be her.

But then they had kept talking and she hadn't heard everything.

A few minutes later, Georgey walked—no, strutted—into the living room like he was hot stuff. Whatever Tim said to him, it left the boy with a clear case of overinflated ego. Which was almost as dangerous as him with a gun.

"Sit down," she told him.

"Let me just check the perimeter," he said with a swagger.

Summer rolled her eyes, but she didn't stop him as he checked the windows and locks on the doors. When he was done, he sat on the edge of the couch, his body tense and his eyes restless. It was as if he expected to be attacked by the creatures of the night at any moment.

Which would've sounded ridiculous about an hour and a half ago. But now? She didn't know anything. Not anymore.

"We need to figure out what we're going to do," she told him in her most grown-up voice.

"I'm going to keep you safe," Georgey said.

"I was talking more about the long-term rather than the next three hours," she said, unable to keep the ice out of her voice. "You're a minor and I prefer you not handle guns."

"I know how to shoot." Just like that, Georgey's swagger was subsumed beneath a teenage boy's attitude.

"I appreciate that the sheriff told you to keep me safe, but that gun better be under his pillow and not tucked in your waistband."

"You're not my mom, you know."

This again. Summer knew she had long months, if not years, of this awaiting her if she took custody of

69

this child. "No, I'm not. But I have rules. You will watch your mouth around me and you will not pack firearms. Put it back. *Now*." Then she waited to see what he would do.

Georgey held her gaze for the longest moment—just long enough she was certain he was going to defy her openly. Then he got to his feet. "Your rules suck," he muttered under his breath as he headed back down the hallway.

When he came back, he did not sit at the edge of the couch and look vigilant. Instead, he slumped back, crossed his arms and scowled. She had her work cut out for her.

"What would you like to see happen, George?"

"What do you mean? And why do you call me George? My name is Georgey."

She didn't answer immediately, holding the silence just long enough the boy began to squirm. "I called you Georgey when you were three. But you're not a little boy anymore. However," she added before he could shoot off his mouth again, "I will call you whatever you'd like, since we're going to be together for the foreseeable future."

Georgey managed to look both worried and defiant at the same time. "So I'm stuck with you? Is that it?"

She shrugged, trying to look nonchalant. "You can stay here. I don't remember very much about your mother, although the Sheriff has made it clear he would prefer not to turn you over to her." She leaned toward him. "I'm sorry about your grandmother, but I don't know that she'll be able to take care of you anymore."

The look that passed over Georgey's face was brief but intense. It told Summer what she needed to know—the boy truly did care about his grandma. "Whatever," he muttered.

"It's not *whatever*," she retorted. "I'm willing to wait and see how she does. I can't tell you if she's going to get better or not. But I can tell you what I expect from you. You will go back to school. If you stay here, I still expect you to get your high school diploma or your GED. If you come with me, I will personally enroll you in my school and keep an eye on you."

Georgey made a *pfft* noise, but he didn't say anything smart-ass. Summer took that as a good sign. She went on, "Right now, I live in a one-bedroom apartment. If you come with me, we'll move into a two-bedroom apartment. You will have your own space. But there will be rules. No firearms, no weapons in general, no drugs and no alcohol. You'll maintain a C average or higher for your grades."

"Yay, more rules," he mumbled.

"In exchange," she continued as if he hadn't spoken, "I will provide you with clothes that fit, food to eat, and a safe place to sleep. We might be able to negotiate about transportation. A bike is fine for the summer, but you might need a car for the winter. Minneapolis is cold."

She could tell Georgey was trying not to look excited. His studious boredom, however, cracked around the edges as his eyes widened at the mention of a car. "I, uh, I don't have my driver's license. But I do know how to drive."

She leveled her sternest glare at him. "Yes, I saw

the part where you'd stolen a truck. If you live under my roof, you will follow the law. Being arrested will revoke any privileges you have. If you get a car, you would lose it immediately. Do I make myself clear?"

"Yeah." Georgey started tapping his fingers on his forearm. "You got a boyfriend or something?"

"Nope. I don't even have a cat." She smiled, and he almost cracked one back. Then she took a deep breath and told him what she didn't want to. "There's one complication with this potential plan—my mother. She's not a big fan of our father and I don't think she's going to be…happy to see you."

Georgey stared at her, looking young. She could almost see the toddler he'd once been. "Would we live with her?"

"No." For the first time, Summer realized that her mother might actually disown her.

Was that a risk she was willing to take?

Georgey leaned forward, his elbows on his knees. "I don't like school," he warned her.

"I don't care," she replied. "What do you think you're going to do with your life if you don't have a high school degree? I'll be risking a lot to bring you home with me—do you understand that? I don't have a lot of money and I'm sure my mother won't help. But we are family and once upon a time, I promised our father that I would look after you. I keep my promises. What I'm asking from you is a promise to do the same. You get good grades, you don't get kicked out of school and you don't break the law. You might have to get a job to help out. And in exchange I'll take care of you. I'll help you figure out what you're going to do for the rest of your life. This is the deal, Georgey.

Because Sheriff Tim seems to think that if I leave you here, you're going to be spending a lot more time in a jail cell. So which is it going to be? Are you going to give up? Or are you going to try to work for something?"

Silence settled over the living room. She had no idea if she had gotten through to him. It was pretty clear the concept of living within a certain set of rules was daunting to Georgey. How long had he been running completely wild. Had his grandmother been able to do anything for him?

Summer harbored no illusions about what would happen if she took him home with her. There might be a grace period where he tried—but sooner or later, he'd rub up against one of the rules and he'd push back. He was ten years younger than she was, but he had a good four inches on her.

He'd never been arrested for assaulting anyone, though. She'd checked.

Finally she said, "You can think about it, you know. I had to give up my summer teaching job to come out here and Tim said he might be able to get me a part-time job teaching GED classes. We could be here until school starts in the fall. But you've got to stay out of trouble. You finish up at the clinic and you do whatever other community service chores Tim assigns to you and you show me that you can follow the rules and that I won't regret taking you in and then we can talk about a car when you get to Minneapolis. Understood?"

The car was going to be stretching it. But Georgey nodded. If a car was the carrot she needed to get him to behave, then that was what it took.

"Now," she said in a softer voice. "I know all about your arrest record but I don't know very much about you. If I'm going to be cooking you dinner, you better tell me what kind of food you like."

***

Nights like this made Tim wish he worked in a nice big city with a nice modern jail that had whole cellblocks on separate floors instead of three cells, all within shouting distance of his desk. Because every cell was full and there was a shit-ton of shouting going on.

He had the Killerz in the far left cell and the Warriors in the far right one. The unconscious ones from both gangs were in the middle. Tim scowled at Nobody's handiwork. He didn't think anybody was on the verge of death in there, but he wasn't sure.

"Man, you can't hold me!" Levi shouted. A few of the Warriors made some unflattering comments about Levi's parentage and if Tim hadn't been worried about having to repair the damage on his own dime, he would've fired a couple of shots into the ceiling just to shut them all up.

If they didn't settle down soon, ceilings be damned.

Tim looked over at Jack. "Did you get an ETA?"

Jack shook his head. He'd called in the state troopers and made contact with his FBI handler about the Los Perros lead, but it was two in the morning and no one was in a great big hurry to get out to the White Sandy.

It was going to be a *hell* of a long night.

Jack leaned forward and said quietly, so that only Tim could hear him, "We need Nobody."

Tim nodded. The only way these idiots would sit down and shut up was if Nobody was scaring the hell out of them.

"See if he'll come in," Tim said.

Jack got up, which drew the attention of multiple gang bangers. They turned their attention from Levi to Jack, and while the deputy was normally hard to ruffle, tonight he'd taken some direct fire and had been grazed on the shoulder. It hadn't done wonders for his mood. He threw open the door and turned around to glare at the prisoners.

Then he turned off the light.

Everyone got blissfully quiet as they waited to see what Jack was going to do. He walked back to his desk and turned on a lamp. Almost everyone's gaze followed Jack, which meant they missed Nobody slipping in like a shadow. It wasn't until the leader of the Warriors, Chuck, stepped forward and told Jack where he could put his lamp—only to be yanked against the bars so hard Tim heard something snap— that everyone realized Jack and Tim were not alone anymore.

Everyone—except for Chuck—shut the hell up and backed against the far wall, out of the way of Nobody's long reach. Chuck made a noise that was half groan, half scream. Tim took advantage of the silence and said, "There are worse things in this world than being locked up in jail for the night. I'd be happy to let any of you go right now. But once you're no longer a guest of the White Sandy police, you're on your own, aren't you?"

Nobody released his grip on Chuck and shoved him back. The leader fell on his ass and scooted back as if he'd seen the face of the devil himself.

No one requested to be released.

"Now," Tim went on. "I hope everyone has a clear understanding of how far we will go to keep this reservation a safe and law abiding place to live."

"This is police brutality," somebody muttered. It sounded like it came from the Killerz cell.

"How can that be? Jack and I are the only police on this reservation," he informed them at large. "We had no knowledge of any other force. There are no other deputies and no other sanctioned law enforcement members. Anything else you're seeing is most likely a figment of your imagination."

"Goddamn *sica*," someone else whispered.

An electric charge passed around the room, making Tim's teeth chatter with the force of the power. Jesus, Nobody wasn't going to turn into a fireball, was he? Tim had been on the receiving end of some of his electric shocks before, but this was crazy.

What only made it worse was that even Tim wasn't exactly sure where Nobody was in the room.

"Can you turn the lights back on?" a small, scared voice asked. If Tim hadn't been one hundred percent sure Georgey was back at his place with Summer, he would've guessed it was the boy. But it wasn't. It was the kid everyone called Shorty. And he probably wasn't older than fifteen. "Blaine isn't moving," Shorty went on. He sounded like he was about to start crying.

"Shut up, Shorty," someone snapped. It sounded like Levi.

76

Tim tilted the shade of his lamp so it shone where he thought Shorty was standing. The kid looked all of twelve surrounded by older, tougher men.

"Here's the thing," he said to the kid. "The doctor is a good woman who won't take any of your shit and Clarence doesn't like idiots. I'm trying to figure out why I should bother to wake either of them up in the middle of the night to take care of any of you." Shorty looked stricken. "What did you think was going to happen? You were all going to miss? No. You went there to hurt someone. And someone got hurt. This is what happens when you declare war on your own people. You watch them die and you know it was your fault."

Now the kid was crying and Tim felt bad. He tried to think—who the hell was Blaine? But he drew a blank.

Normally, this was the point where Jack would jump in and be the good cop. Tim was the bad cop and Nobody was the scary not-cop. But Jack was still pissed about being shot and he made no move to smooth over the truth of the situation. Instead, he sat there and glared.

Still, Tim couldn't exactly have a bunch of dead prisoners on his hand. It would look bad. So after another minute—and he made damn sure it was a full minute—he said, "I'll see what I can do. But I hear one lewd or rude comment to any medical professional who bothers to show up to save your sorry hides, and I will turn the lights off and walk out. Do I make myself clear?"

Just in case he hadn't, Tim felt a little burst of the electricity coming off of Nobody. Apparently, the man was standing by the front door.

The only sound was of Shorty sniffling. Tim remembered telling Summer that it depended on the kid and it depended on the crime, but he'd had other kids sleeping on his couch. It wasn't a lie—but it wasn't entirely the truth either.

He looked at Jack and nodded. Jack got up and walked slowly to the front of the room, and although Tim kept his eyes on the door, he didn't see Nobody slip out. But when Jack flipped on the light, there were only two people in the room who weren't in a cell.

"Now, we can do this the easy way," Tim told the stunned group, "or we can do it the hard way. And we all know what the hard way is, don't we?" A few people turned their backs on him, refusing to see him or Jack. That was fine. "Shorty, come to the front of the cell."

Tim wanted to go home. He wanted to see if Summer was tucked in his bed, if she'd wake up when he stuck his head into the room to make sure she was all right. He wanted to make sure Georgey hadn't done anything stupid, like sleep with the gun tucked into his waistband. He did not want to spend the next several hours calling parents and grandparents and dealing with state troopers and FBI agents and filling out accident reports explaining how some people's arms might have gotten broken while in custody.

But he didn't have much of a choice at this point. This was the job.

His job.

Chapter Seven

Summer woke with a start. For a moment, she didn't know where she was. She didn't recognize the room, the bed, anything. She heard a *thunk* that came from outside the bedroom door.

Tim.

It all came back to her. She was in Tim's house, sleeping in his bed—waiting on him to come home. She blinked at the clock—6:18. Was he just getting home? Was everything okay?

She slipped out of bed and cautiously opened the door. The smell of coffee hit her nose the same moment she heard soft voices.

"…Shoot anyone?" That was Georgey.

"Not fatally," Tim replied. He sounded bone tired. "You were right about Levi. Do me a favor, kid—don't tell anyone else what you told me."

"What happened?" As tired as Tim sounded, Georgey sounded equally excited. If not more so.

"You know what happened. Jack and I met them from opposite angles and Nobody drifted around the perimeter, picking off the easy ones." There was a pause. "It's good you weren't there, kid. There were a lot of shots fired. It got messy."

Summer gave silent thanks Georgey had been sulking *here*.

"Did you see who shot you?"

Oh, Lord—he'd been shot? Summer flung herself into the room. "Are you okay?" she demanded. Then she stopped.

Because Sheriff Tim Means was leaning against the kitchen counter without a shirt on. His pants were unbuckled and the top button was undone, giving her a glimpse of the line of dark hair that dipped below his fly.

Her brain was having trouble processing his chest. There were small scars and a few larger ones crisscrossing his biceps and chest. He was lean and muscled and she couldn't believe she'd *ever* thought this man had a beer gut because there wasn't a spare ounce of fat on him.

Tim looked at her. He lifted one eyebrow, but he made no move to buckle up or grab a shirt.

That was when she realized he also didn't have any open gunshot wounds on him.

"Summer, check this out," Georgey said with unabashed adoration in his voice. "I mean, this is so cool!"

Summer could barely tear her gaze away from Tim's chest, but she didn't have much choice when Georgey held the vest up in front of her. It took a moment to comprehend what she was seeing—the same vest Tim had worn last night, except now there was a dent in the front almost two inches wide.

She stared at that dent, then her gaze jolted back to Tim's chest. She stepped forward and saw what she'd missed the first time—the darker red spot under his left pec. Already, it was deepening to angry purple. "Are you all right?" she asked.

"Been better. Been worse."

She looked up at him and saw the dark circles under his eyes.

"How about you? You have a quiet night?"

She stared at him but he just sipped his coffee, as if this were another Saturday morning and not him coming close to being killed in a gang war. "I was worried about you," she admitted.

That got a smirk out of him. "I'm not the one you should be worried about." He broke her gaze and turned his attention back to Georgey, who'd spread the vest out on the kitchen table. "Jack got grazed by a bullet, but it was a scratch. I didn't see who shot me, but there were only a few people with guns."

Summer stared at his chest again. "You need to ice that." Without waiting for an answer, she pulled open the freezer door. He had one tray of ice. She started rummaging through the cabinets, hoping to find a baggie or something, but in the end she had to settle for a washcloth. She dumped half the ice in, tied the ends together and turned back to where Tim watched her with an amused smile on his face.

"Here," she said, pressing the ice pack against his chest. His bare chest.

His gaze dipped and Summer realized she was still in her pajamas. Which meant she didn't have on a bra.

It was at that exact moment her nipples decided to join the conversation, tightening underneath the T-shirt until she could feel them pointing through the fabric. Tim's gaze snapped back up, his pupils widening as he stared at her.

"Can I really ride along with you next time you

do this?" Georgey said, apparently blissfully unaware Tim and Summer were engaged in something deeper than first aid.

"What? No," Summer said quickly. "You are absolutely not allowed to go along to a shootout and that is final, young man."

"*Aww*," Georgey started to whine.

But Tim cut him off. "Your sister's right. You'd just get yourself killed."

"Would not," Georgey protested. "I know how to shoot. I can handle a gun."

Summer twisted so she could stare at the young man without letting go of the ice pack. Which meant she was leaning up against the counter, more or less nestled against Tim's side. "Don't make me ground you," she said. Then Tim's arm came to rest around her waist and whatever else she was going to say got lost on the way to her mouth.

"Kid," Tim said in a stern voice, "Jack and I are both ex-military and I've got a degree in criminal justice. It's not enough to know how to handle a gun. If you'd been there last night, either somebody would've killed you or you would've killed somebody and trust me, that's not something to be taken lightly. You want to be a warrior, you have to earn that right."

Georgey opened his mouth to shoot off a smart-ass reply, no doubt, but for the first time, he seemed to notice they were both in the room—together. He almost physically recoiled as Tim's hand fell away from Summer's waist.

Tim reached up and pulled her hand, with the frozen pack, away from his chest. "Put this back in the freezer for me, will you? I'm going to take a shower.

Then I need to sleep for a couple hours. Do you think you can get Georgey to the Clinic so he can finish working on the window?"

Frankly, she wasn't entirely sure she could find the Clinic. But compared to Tim's problems, that seemed like a minor issue. "Will you be okay?"

He shrugged and, in the process, stepped away from her. "Just need some sleep. A few hours and I'll be as good as new."

Summer eyed the deepening bruise on his chest. She had her doubts about that, but she said, "We'll get out of your way, then." She turned to Georgey. "Do we need to swing by your grandma's house and get some of your things?"

She realized immediately it was not the right thing to say. Georgey's cheeks shot bright red. "I don't have anything else," he said.

"Oh." She felt stupid. She'd had students who were poor before. She should've known he wouldn't have this huge wardrobe or a bunch of stuff to pack. "Then we'll need to start a list," she said because she had to say something. "But," she hurried to add when Georgey's eyes lit up, "you still have to pay Tim back for the window or however that works. You're on your own for that."

***

It took longer than Tim expected for Georgey and Summer to get out of the house. Georgey spent another twenty minutes in the bathroom, then Summer had to shower. During which time, Tim had to *not* think about Summer being in the shower.

83

He also had to not think about the way she'd looked when she'd burst out of the bedroom this morning, her hair tousled and her face creased from the pillow.

He'd wanted to do nothing more than pull her into his arms, tell her he'd had a long night, and lead her right back to bed. He was hurting and she'd looked like the best kind of painkiller—warm and soft and more than enough to take his mind off the hurt.

Then he'd seen her nipples tighten under her T-shirt and she'd curled up against his side and what little grip he had on his control had started to shake.

No, he'd never given his bed up to anyone else. But for her? Yeah, he'd make an exception. Right now he was too tired to do anything but sleep, but when the Tylenol kicked in and he'd gotten some sleep?

He wanted to find out exactly what it took to make her nipples tighten up again. He wanted to find out how those nipples felt in his mouth and he wanted to know what noises she'd make when he sucked.

Instead, he stood in his kitchen and drank more coffee and prayed he'd get at least two hours of sleep before his phone rang again.

Finally, though, they were gone. Tim took a hot shower and then got out Summer's homemade ice pack and wrapped it against his chest with an elastic bandage. Technically, he'd lied. He knew damn well he wasn't going to be all right after a couple of hours asleep. His chest throbbed and he knew from experience he'd be sore for days. Better than being dead, of course, but still a pain in the ass—or the chest, as it were. He sprawled out on the bed on his back, a towel underneath his ribs to catch the melted ice. Then he closed his eyes.

Normally, Tim could fall sleep at the drop of a hat. It was a life skill, after all. You slept when you could and worked when you had to.

But he hadn't counted on the lingering smell of Summer Collins in his bed. The pillowcase held the faintest whiff of vanilla and something else—the unique scent of Summer.

He was bad at flirting. He'd never been good at it and he was way out of practice. Still, even an old man like him knew that when a woman looked at him like that and held ice against his chest when there was nothing wrong with his arm—that was some kind of flirtation. What he didn't know was, when she'd turned to look at Georgey and stepped into his arms and he'd put his hand around her waist just because she'd felt so good against him, was that flirting, too? Or was that the exhaustion talking?

She hadn't twisted out of his grasp or pushed his hand away, but she had told him in no uncertain terms she was going to check on his bruising again later tonight and he had better sleep while they were gone.

It was a promise he hoped like hell she was going to keep.

***

Normally, Tim's sleep was blackness. He didn't dream, or if he did, he didn't remember it. But today, odd, disjointed images floated around his mind. Bodies moving together and apart and he had a gun—he always had a gun. There was something he wanted to be doing, something that seemed important, but he had the gun in his hand and he couldn't reach the body next to him. Whoever it was, she danced and spun just out of his grasp, an impression more than a person.

Weird, he thought. And he was cognizant enough to know that thought in and of itself was unusual.

Then something touched his shoulder and cut through the weird dream. Instinct took over. He reached up and grabbed the wrists of the person who'd managed to sneak into his house, and rolled. Before he even got his eyes open, he had the intruder trapped underneath him and he was trying to reach for the gun under his pillow. Except it wasn't there. Dammit.

"Oh!" A soft feminine voice squeaked from under him.

His eyelids were heavy and he realized he'd been asleep. "Who are you," he demanded as he forced his eyes open.

That was when he realized he'd pinned Summer to his bed. He had her by her wrists and her body was warm and soft underneath his.

Oh, shit.

"Tim?" Her eyes were wide—the kind of eyes a man could get lost in—and she should have been terrified. But he didn't think she was. Maybe a little alarmed. He couldn't really blame her for that.

"Tim?" she asked again and he realized he hadn't answered her yet.

His brain felt like sludge and he was vaguely aware this was the worst thing he had done all day. Probably all week. "What are you doing here? Where's Georgey?"

Amazingly, instead of kicking and screaming and trying to throw him off her—all things she should've done—one corner of her mouth quirked up. "He's at the

Clinic," she said in a remarkably calm voice, given the circumstances. "Jack was there, getting some stitches. He told me to tell you…" Her voice drifted off.

Tim tried not to think about the way her body was molding itself to his. *Soft*. She was so soft.

"He said the state troopers were watching the prisoners, but you need to get down there sooner rather than later. I gathered they didn't want Jack bleeding all over the place," she added, her smile growing slightly. "Apparently he tried to call you, but you didn't answer. So he's keeping an eye on Georgey and I offered to come check on you."

He'd slept through the phone? And the state troopers were taking over his station? Tim winced, which she took the wrong way.

"Are you okay?" She pulled one of her wrists free from his hand and then she was touching him. Her fingers slid down his side, over his ribs until they hit the bandage and he almost lost what little self-control he was hanging onto, because she was touching him and looking at him with those beautiful eyes and he wasn't going to make it.

"Your ice melted," she told him.

"Yeah." Great. He sounded like an idiot, but he couldn't seem to get his brain or his mouth to function.

Something in her eyes changed. "I'm sorry I woke you up," she said, her voice growing even quieter.

"It's okay," he said, mentally ordering his brain to get with it. "I should get up anyway."

Neither of them moved. He still had her head bracketed with his forearms, her one hand pinned over her head. She was still lightly tracing his ribs.

And he was going to kiss her. It probably wasn't

87

the right thing to do. It definitely wasn't the smart thing to do. There were a lot of really good reasons why he shouldn't cross this line with her. But he was having trouble thinking of any of them right now.

All he could think about was the way her body fit against his, how pretty she was.

How she wasn't clawing his eyes out or calling him names.

She moved first. Her free hand left his bandage behind and skimmed over his chest, then up his neck. She stroked the side of his face and tucked a hank of his hair behind his ear. Then, somehow, her fingers were tangled in his hair and she was pulling him down to her.

"Summer," he whispered against her skin and then he was kissing her. Maybe this was just a hyper-real dream, because the feel of Summer, the way her mouth moved against his, the way she opened and sighed into him—this couldn't be real. If he was asleep, he sure as hell didn't want to wake up.

Summer's tongue traced his lips and he groaned. He shifted and she shifted with him, her legs wrapping around his and pulling him down harder into her. God, how long had it been? Months? Years? He couldn't remember. All he knew was it had been too long since he'd been tangled up with a woman in this bed, lips and hands and legs everywhere.

He shifted again, releasing her wrist and propping himself up so he could touch her. He cupped her breast and squeezed—maybe not as gently as he should have, because she gasped and broke the kiss. But before he could apologize for being too rough, she arched into his touch, her head thrown back against the pillow and her mouth open.

"Pretty," he managed to get out and then his hips moved without his explicit permission, grinding his dick against her. "So damn pretty," he said again because it was true and also because he didn't want her to leave. Not now.

"Tim…"

In the other room, his phone rang.

They both froze, eyes wide.

"I'm supposed to be checking on you," she whispered.

"I'm supposed to be down at the station," he replied.

Neither one moved. The phone kept ringing.

Summer's lips twisted into a smile Tim hoped was more amused than anything else. Then she shifted and put her hands on his chest. With a gentle push, she said, "Here. Sit back and let me look at you."

Tim lifted an eyebrow at her but did as she asked, sitting on his heels. She scooted into a cross-legged position, still close enough to touch. But he didn't. The moment was over and his brain had stopped misfiring. He shouldn't be fooling around with the guardian of someone in his custody. Not if he wanted to and not even if she wanted to.

She started to unwrap the bandage around his chest. The ice had melted completely and the whole thing was sopping. He glanced down and saw her shirt was wet too, from where he'd been laying on her. "Sorry," he said as she worked.

"For what?" Somehow she managed to sound like this was just another day. Maybe it was for her.

But it wasn't for him. "For…" He was pretty sure there were several things he needed to apologize for.

But he wasn't as awake as he'd like to be. Not yet, anyway. "I sort of tackled you." It could have been worse, he realized. His gun wasn't under the pillow where it normally was. If he'd managed to get a grip on his pistol, he didn't think the encounter would've ended with kissing. Thank God for small favors.

She shrugged. "I sort of snuck up on you while you were sleeping. Your self-preservation instincts are hardwired, aren't they? Oh," she gasped as the bandage fell away and she got a good look at his chest.

"How bad is it?" Tim tried to glance down but he didn't have a good angle on it and he couldn't bend to get a better one without his ribs screaming in protest.

"It's…" She looked up at him and he thought she looked green around the gills. "Maybe you should go to the clinic," she finished.

Tim took a couple deep breaths but there was no stabbing pain. Just the dull ache. He could live with a dull ache. "I don't think anything's broken and if it is, all they can do is wrap it."

Her gaze dropped back to what must be some truly spectacular bruising. "Are you sure?"

It was odd, having someone worry about him. Sure, Jack worried about him—but only to the extent of whether Tim could still do his job.

No one was ever worried about *him*. And just like that, he wanted to kiss her more. Harder.

The phone rang again. "Dammit," he mumbled. He leaned down as best he could without losing his balance or making his ribs scream and he pressed his lips to hers. But quickly. "I have to go." He scooted off the bed and made sure his legs were under him.

"At least let me wrap your chest," she said as he

slid his closet door open and reached for a clean uniform shirt. "If nothing else, you need the extra padding."

He half turned to look at her. She climbed off the bed and waited. His first instinct was to say he didn't need any extra padding. But the half turn had strained his ribs and besides, he was finding it increasingly difficult to say no to her. "Okay."

He headed to the bathroom, where he'd left his first aid kit spread all over the counter. He dug around until he found another elastic bandage and handed it to her. Then he turned to face the mirror and got a good look at his body.

The bruise was stunning, almost the size of a soccer ball. It started below his left pectoral muscle and wrapped around his side. On some level, he was aware he should hurt more than he did. Gunshots hurt like a bitch. Plus there wasn't exactly a budget for replacing his dented armor. He was also aware that, if he had newer equipment, he might not have a bruise that looked this bad.

"Arms up," Summers said in an efficient voice. He did as he was told and lifted his arms up as high as they would go. The right one went farther than the left. Summer sighed, which made him smile.

No doubt, she was thinking to herself, *Men*.

"It's not as bad as it looks," he reassured her.

"So you said." She made a *tsking* noise as she wrapped the bandage around his chest. "Does this happen often?"

Tim watched her in the mirror. The fuzziness of sleep was fading from his mind, but the urge to kiss her? Still there. "Which *this*? The part where I get shot

91

or the part where I pin a beautiful woman to my bed and kiss her?"

She paused, her shoulders tense. He shouldn't have said that. He wasn't sure if it was the nap or what, but this was not normally how he rolled.

She continued to rewrap his chest. "Both, I suppose," she said in a pinched voice and he knew he'd embarrassed her.

"I don't normally pin women to my bed. I didn't realize it was you and again, I'm sorry I scared you." He did not, however, apologize for kissing her. He wasn't sure he would even if she punched him in the ribs.

She adjusted the bandage and tucked in the loose ends. "And getting shot?"

He tried to shrug but it pulled, so he stopped. "It happens. There are plenty of people who aren't happy to see me. That's nothing new."

Summer stood back and admired her handiwork. Then, in the mirror, she met his gaze. She looked like she wanted to say something—and God, Tim wanted her to say something. He wanted to know he hadn't scared her. No, that wasn't enough—he wanted to know she'd wanted him to keep kissing her, that he hadn't misunderstood the way she kissed him back.

"I don't really know what I'm doing," she said in a small voice. "I don't think I belong here."

Tim was not the most sensitive guy. But he was pretty sure he caught her meaning. She didn't know what she was doing kissing *him*. "You do," he told her. "You can always come back to the rez." Because if she came back...

Tim was getting ahead of himself. He hadn't even made it through today. And he had a lot of daylight left.

They stood there for a moment longer, neither of them moving. This seemed to be a trend. Normally, Tim was a man of action. But not when Summer was around. He could stand here and look at her all day.

She made a movement, like she wanted to step into him but then thought better of it. "Will I see you again later?" she asked.

To hell with that. Tim lifted his right arm—the good one—and draped it over her shoulder, pulling her into him. "I have to deal with the state troopers and finish processing last night's shootout. But after that— I sure hope so."

She leaned into him, her body warm against his. It was the sort of touch that seemed to say more kissing could happen. More *everything* could happen.

What he wouldn't give to pull her right back into the bed and curl up with her.

God, he liked holding her. They looked good together. Her head came up to his chin and, as she leaned against his shoulder, he found himself wanting to make all sorts of promises to her, how he'd keep her safe and keep her loved.

"You didn't, you know. Scare me."

He looked down at her. "Do you normally have men pounce on you like that?"

She shook her head. "I'm pretty sure that was the first time."

"Still, I'll try not to do it again. The pouncing, that is."

Something in her eyes changed—deepened. She reached up and stroked his cheek. "Right. No more pouncing."

His heart began to pound because that sounded

almost like an invitation. What the hell. She was already in his arms. He was already in deep. "I'm going to kiss you again."

"Oh." Her eyes fluttered and she tilted her head back—and the damned phone rang again.

Tim groaned and Summer stepped away from him. "Tonight?"

Hell, yeah. "Tonight," he agreed.

"Good." She stood on her tiptoes to press her lips against his—another short kiss that held more promise than heat. "Now go."

"Yes, ma'am." So he went.

But he was coming back tonight.

Chapter Eight

Summer was supposed to be paying attention to her brother and the work he was doing at the Clinic. Sure, her eyes were pointed in Georgey's general direction. But that wasn't what she saw.

Instead, she saw Tim Means above her, sleep thick in his eyes and his body heavy on hers. She saw the moment when he'd realized who she was—and the moment when he hadn't rolled off her. She relived touching him, the way his eyelids had fluttered and he'd shivered—actually *shivered*. Because of her.

And that kiss... God, the feeling of his lips against hers, the weight of his body pressing down on her? The way he'd stared into her eyes in the bathroom and told her he was going to kiss her again later?

She touched her lips and smiled. So the whole summer-fling thing was a go, it seemed. There was only one problem with it.

Georgey. He was dripping sweat and every time he moved, Summer got that much closer to hosing him off. Why did teen boys smell so much? She honestly couldn't tell if that was just boy sweat or if he'd layered on some body spray to intentionally smell that bad. Whatever it was, Summer was surprised the staff of the Clinic hadn't said something. The kid was a one-man health hazard.

Despite the eye-watering odor, Georgey got the window in. Clarence, the big male nurse, came over and looked over Georgey's work because Summer didn't have a clue if the glass was in correctly or not.

She half expected Georgey to cop an attitude with Clarence, but he didn't. Instead, it seemed like the kid hung on Clarence's approval. He looked nervous—although that could've been because he didn't want to redo the window. Or because he was afraid of Clarence.

Clarence took his sweet time studying the window. He *hmm-ed* and *uh-huh-ed* a couple times until Georgey apparently couldn't take it anymore.

"Well?" the boy demanded.

Clarence gave him a dull look. "You got someplace else you need to be?" he said in a voice that got perilously close to booming.

"No, sir," Georgey quickly answered, dropping his chin.

Summer hid her smile behind her hand. But she didn't dare interrupt Clarence. He reminded her of the assistant principal at her high school, Mr. Schunking, who also coached the wrestling team.

"Not bad, for a kid," Clarence finally pronounced in serious tones. He tapped on the glass and Summer held her breath—what if the whole thing flipped out?

But it held.

"Now what?" Georgey said. "I fixed it. I'm done, right?"

Clarence snorted and glanced over at Summer. "You got anything you need him for?"

"Um…" She hadn't gotten that far. She hadn't realized Georgey was going to get the window done today and she'd been too busy thinking about kissing the sheriff.

"Because my wife could use a hand next door. At the Child Care Center," Clarence explained when it became obvious Summer no idea what he was talking about. He sighed. "Dr. Mitchell's sister runs it with my wife—it's the only daycare on the rez. But Tammy's seven months pregnant and she can't chase the kids around." He swung his massive head back around to Georgey. "Can you play soccer?"

"It's not complicated," Georgey said as he rolled his eyes. "It's just kicking a ball around."

"So you think you can handle it?" Clarence replied, unperturbed by the attitude. Then again, Summer found it hard to believe there was much that bothered the big man.

Georgey looked at Clarence suspiciously, then he turned to Summer and waited. For permission, she realized. Was he tacitly agreeing Summer was in charge? Well, wasn't that something?

"That's fine." Because frankly, she wasn't sure what else to do with the boy just yet—and she wasn't ready to go back to Tim's house, either. Not with Georgey in tow. How was she supposed to act with Tim while Georgey was hanging around? "Congratulations," she added to Clarence. "Is this your first one?"

The big man's whole face softened into a wide smile. "We also have a six-year-old—my adopted son."

We are all family. Summer couldn't help the pang of jealousy that went through her. She glanced at Georgey and saw he was staring at the ground.

What would their lives had been like if their stepparents had welcomed them into each other's homes? If they'd been a family, no matter what?

Clarence walked over to the door that separated the Clinic from the daycare. "Babe?" he said in a quiet voice. "Georgey will help out."

"Oh, good," an equally soft voice replied.

Summer peeked around Clarence and saw that most of the kids were on cots—but not all of them were sleeping. A few older kids were either sitting at a small table or flopping around on the floor, reading. The room was an organized mess, with art on the walls and toys shoved onto shelves and in bins. But the whole room felt warm and fun.

Clarence introduced Summer to his wife. Tammy Thunder was a small, plump and very pregnant young woman with a sweet smile—the kind of woman who was so obviously a natural with children it made Summer wonder if she could ever measure up.

Which was sort of the wrong way to go about it. Summer could handle the bigger kids. It was just babies who made her nervous.

"It's good to meet you," Tammy said in that quiet voice. She maneuvered over to a ragged-looking couch and sat down. Summer followed, but Georgey hung back by the door, looking awkward. "If you don't mind, I thought I'd have Georgey run a soccer game. I just can't keep up these days and Melonie had to go to court this afternoon."

"Melonie?"

Tammy nodded. "My boss—Dr. Mitchell's sister. Oh, and Nobody's wife. I heard you met him?"

Summer blushed. "I...did? I guess?"

Tammy laughed. "That's all most people can say. He's hard to pin down." She gave Summer a long look.

Summer began to squirm and she wasn't sure why. Tammy was, hands down, the easiest person to talk to on this reservation.

"Why is your boss in court?"

"Melonie? Oh, she's an advocate. Tim arrested a couple of kids who were underage and she's shepherding them through the system, making sure they have some place to go if they make bail." She looked up to Georgey, who still looked horribly uncomfortable. "Including Shorty and Blaine."

Embarrassment flamed over his cheeks. "Yeah, I heard."

"Blaine had a concussion and a broken jaw. Did you know that?"

Georgey shook his head and Summer had to turn to look at Tammy. Oh, she was a tough nut. Underneath that warm, soft exterior was a woman who took no crap. Summer liked her immensely.

"Clarence fixed him up," Tammy went on. "That could have been you, you know."

Georgey slumped against the doorframe in surrender. "I know," he said, sounding miserable.

A couple kids who'd been doing a lousy job pretending to be asleep sat up and stared openly. One little boy still had his thumb in his mouth.

"Well!" Tammy said in a bright voice. A few more kids sat up. "I think it's time for snacks and then Georgey's going to play soccer with us! I think we'll have Jamie lead one team and Georgey the other!"

That got almost everyone up and cheering and

suddenly the whole place was a swarming mass of excited children. Summer sat on the edge, answering all sorts of nosy questions from overenthusiastic kids without a filter. Who was she? What was her name? Was she really an Indian? Was she going to play soccer, too?

Which was how she found herself maybe not playing soccer, but refereeing the game. Jamie turned out to be the oldest kid at the center, maybe ten or eleven. And he was the son of the mysterious Nobody—adopted, Tammy told her in quiet tones from where she sat in the shade, keeping an eye on the babies.

"Are they related?"

Tammy shook her head, but then added, "We're all related somewhere along the line, you know?"

Summer remembered Clarence had adopted Tammy's son, too. The whole thing was so unusual. She'd encountered more than her fair share of relatives who refused to take a child into their home for whatever reasons. She'd seen kids get shunted off to foster care, alone and unwanted. Black, white—it hadn't really mattered.

But here, relatives stepped up. Non-relatives stepped up. People took care of the kids—or they tried, anyway. Summer looked at Georgey as he coached his team of kids, ranging from ages three to nine, up and down the field. Was she really it?

But then she thought of Tim Means. He'd had Georgey sleeping on his couch rather than leaving him in a cell. He'd fronted the money for the glass to replace the broken window.

"He's doing well," Tammy observed as Georgey yelled, "No, no—the other way—the other way!" as a little kid headed for his own goal.

Summer didn't even try to hide her smile as Georgey went "Argh!" in frustration—but didn't cuss.

"I'm still trying to understand everything," she told Tammy. "Where is his mom?"

Tammy sighed. "I hate it when a kid slips through the cracks. But the thing is, the cracks out here on the rez are so much bigger and there are so many more of them. We do the best we can but before the center here opened, there was no place for kids to go. They either stayed with relatives while their parents worked or they were home alone."

"Seriously? I can't imagine leaving a little kid home alone like that."

"It happens. I just wish we had something for the older kids. Jamie only comes because Melonie adopted him with Nobody. Kids like Shorty and Blaine—Georgey's friends—they're too old for this."

"Great job, buddy!" Georgey yelled when a little boy went the right way and actually managed to kick the ball.

"They don't have anywhere to go or anything safe to do and that's when the gangs get them," Tammy finished sadly. "Tim's doing his best, but one or two men can't hold back the wind."

"Aren't there any after-school programs? Sports or drama?"

Tammy gave her a sad smile. "Most kids drop out before that point."

"Tim mentioned that I might be able to pick up teaching some GED classes at…um…"

"Sinte Gliske? I got my associate's degree from there. That'd be great. If you're going to stay for a while…"

Summer looked out at the gaggle of kids running and kicking and—yes—falling down, all laughing and shouting and having fun. All the kids had the same dark hair, the same brown skin—and the same huge smiles. This was as close to the way she remembered the pow wow had made her feel yet. The sense of community pulled at her.

No, it wasn't community. It was something stronger. Family. "I want to make sure things with Georgey are really settled," she told Tammy. Not to mention things with a certain sheriff. "And Tim said there was a pow wow in a few months. I haven't been to one since I was twelve."

"Where are you staying? With Dr. Mitchell?"

Summer's cheeks got hot. "Um, no—actually, we're staying with Tim. Sheriff Means," she added stupidly, as if Tammy didn't know who Tim was. But suddenly it felt important to talk about Tim in his professional capacity—without all the familiarity. "He'd been letting Georgey sleep on his couch instead of in a cell at the jail," she added.

Tammy opened her mouth to say something, then she winced and rubbed at her belly. "Oof, sorry. Well, I'm sure Tim has things for Georgey to do, but I'm always happy to have him help out. The kids love him."

That much was obvious as someone scored—possibly even on Jamie's team—and everyone lined up to high-five everyone else. Georgey had a small knot of excited children clinging to his legs and he had on what might have been the first real smile Summer had seen on his face.

If she took him back to Minneapolis with her, he'd lose this. He'd lose people like Clarence and

Nobody and Tammy—and, yes, Tim. People who'd go out of their way to give him one more chance, to give him the push he needed.

If she took Georgey back with her, he'd be alone. Not completely alone—but he'd have her and that was it. He'd be cut off from everything he knew, his people and his culture.

Could she do that to her brother?

***

Tim dragged his butt home at a reasonable six-thirty in the evening. Everyone had been processed. Everyone with outstanding warrants had been handed up the food chain. Everyone who was going to make bail had made bail.

The FBI was all over the Los Perros lead and Tim had been effectively iced out. Normally, that might have sat wrong with him—but he was just too damn tired to care.

He hurt and he didn't want to see the inside of the White Sandy police station again for another week. Which wasn't going to happen. He was going to be right back there tomorrow morning sometime between seven and eight.

It was a sad day when twelve solid hours at home was like a vacation.

He should still be at the station. Jack was sleeping on the station couch tonight and—against Tim's better judgment—Nobody was going to be out and about. Tim and Jack were running on less than fumes and if some shit went down, Nobody was going to be the first responder, anyway.

Tim did not like Nobody Bodine. But at this point, the man was acting almost as an unofficial deputy. It went against everything Tim held true about the law and if Nobody stuck anyone in a cell, Tim would have to let them go tomorrow morning.

But he needed sleep. Jack wasn't much better. So Nobody Bodine was the last line of defense on the White Sandy tonight.

Summer's car was parked in front of his house. Just about the only thing that had kept him going today had been the thought of coming home to her and picking up where he'd left off—half naked and wrapped up in each other. All naked would be better but Tim was happy to take what he could get at this point.

He put his shoulder in the door and almost fell in to his house. Okay, so maybe the all-naked thing would have to wait just a little bit longer.

From the kitchen, Summer spun and let out a squeak. She had his oven mitt on her hand and she appeared to be…cooking?

"Tim! You scared me!"

"Sorry," he said, dragging his butt inside and getting the door shut. "The door sticks."

Her lips quirked into a grin. "So I've noticed." She looked at him. "You look exhausted. I'm making dinner, if you can hold out that long."

Tim exhaled a breath he hadn't realized he'd been holding. For years, he'd come home to an empty, dark house. There was something so profoundly normal about Summer waiting for him that he didn't even recognize the emotions that tumbled through him. He just suddenly knew he'd been missing this moment for a long, long time.

"I will eat anything you put in front of me," he told her, slouching into the kitchen chair then sitting up straighter because slouching didn't work with his ribs.

"It's not fancy," she told him. She opened the fridge and the next thing he knew, she set a beer in front of him. "You don't have a lot to work with. Macaroni and cheese, hot dogs, and green beans."

He stared at the beer for what felt like a stupid long time before he looked up at her. She was standing at the edge of the table and she had on this sweet little grin as she watched over him and all of a sudden, he thought, *I could love you.* The words tripped right up to the end of his tongue before he managed to clamp his jaw shut.

That was not the thing he should say right now. Yeah, he liked her and yeah, he'd enjoyed kissing her earlier and okay, yeah, she'd been the one person who'd kept him going all day long. But even in his sorry state, declarations of love just because a pretty woman made him dinner and got him a beer before he realized he wanted one were a bad move.

He opened the beer and took a long pull. "It sounds wonderful," he said sincerely. If he'd come home on his own, he probably would've had a couple hot dogs and fallen into bed. But macaroni and cheese had never sounded so good.

Then he realized they were alone. "Where's Georgey?"

"In the shower," she said in a severe tone. "He smelled like expired aftershave. It was not pretty. But," she went on, sounding far perkier than Tim could achieve at the moment, "he got the window in

105

and done and he spent the afternoon chasing small children around the field with a soccer ball. And he didn't even cuss that much."

Tim felt the grin on his face. "Is that a fact?"

"He's welcome back at the childcare center any time," she told him as she put his oven mitts back on and lifted the pot of boiling water and noodles. She carried it to the sink, but Tim knew he didn't have a strainer. As he watched, she picked up a plate, held it over the lip of the pot, and slowly poured out most of the water.

It was nuts how much watching her do that affected him. Jesus, he must be more tired than he'd thought, but seriously? Not only could he love her, she could fit in his world. He knew she had to have a better life back in Minneapolis—one that included basic kitchen utensils like strainers—but she'd just slipped right into his as if she'd always been here.

He couldn't tell her that, not without sounding like a wacko. But…

Tim pulled himself to his feet. "How long has he been in the shower?" he asked as he walked toward her.

"Fifteen, maybe twenty minutes. He…"

But whatever she'd been about to say faded away as Tim reached her. "Then we've got a few minutes," he said low and close to her ear as he trailed his fingers over her shoulder and down her back.

She carefully set the pot upright so she wouldn't lose all her noodles, then turned. Tim's hands came to rest on her waist and he leaned into her. "I suppose we do," she said in a breathy voice as her arms came around his neck and she tilted her head up.

106

"This counts as later," he told her as he brushed his lips over her forehead and her cheek before working his way toward her mouth.

"Definitely later," she agreed.

God, she felt so good in his arms. The warmth of her body drove the pain in his chest away and the way her mouth moved against his?

He'd been kissing girls since he was at least Georgey's age. But not recently. He'd forgotten how much he loved the soft touch and sweet little noises women made. It was entirely possible he was just too tired and everything was affecting him too much but he didn't think so. He didn't *feel* so.

He had a vague sense this was all out of order. There hadn't been anything that could count as a date, but all he wanted to do was walk her back to the bed and sink into her body.

"Tim," she whispered against his skin as his hands begin to slide up over her ribs. To his ears, it sounded a hell of a lot like *yes*.

"A-*hem*."

Summer jumped in his arms and Tim knew what that sound was. That was a *no*, plain as day.

He half-turned—it was as far as he could go without releasing Summer—and found Georgey staring at them. His hair was wet and his eyes narrowed and he'd crossed his arms in disapproval. For some reason, the combination made Tim want to laugh. Even though the kid was all of a hundred and twenty pounds soaking wet, he was pulling off a very good impression of intimidating at the moment. All because Tim was kissing his sister. A sister he hadn't even remembered having until last week.

107

But Tim didn't laugh.

"Georgey!" Summer gasped, trying to wriggle out of Tim's arms. He didn't let go. "We were just—I mean—um…"

"Heard you got the window in," Tim said, pivoting until Summer was behind him. She was embarrassed, that much he could tell. He wanted to protect her from that. "It better still be there tomorrow."

Georgey looked indignant. "I'm not gonna break it again."

"You might not. But someone else might. And wouldn't that be a shame."

The kid's eyes got even wider. "You mean you'd make me fix it again if someone else breaks it?"

Tim shrugged. "You know how to do it." When Georgey glared at him, Tim said, "It's not much fun when people trash your shit, is it?"

"You're an ass—"

Instead of hiding behind him, Summer stepped around him. Tim shouldn't, but he put his arm back around her waist.

Georgey stumbled on *asshole* so quickly he all but bit himself. "Jerk," he bit off.

Tim grinned at him over Summer's head. "You're coming with me tomorrow morning," he told the kid. "My jail got trashed by a bunch of gangbangers and state troopers and you're still doing community service." When Georgey groaned, Tim added, "If you can make it through the morning without pissing me off, I'll let you go play soccer with the kids again in the afternoon. I heard you did a good job."

Georgey's mouth flopped open, but whatever

remark he'd been about to make died in the face of the compliment. "Oh. It was fun. Better than putting in a window," he mumbled, dropping his gaze. He almost looked like he was blushing.

There was hope for that kid yet. Tim was lifted by a feeling he was doing something right—he and Summer. Together, they were holding Georgey back from the edge of disaster. "Your sister made us dinner. Set the table."

There was a moment where no one moved. Summer hadn't said anything since Georgey stumbled upon them kissing. Georgey looked like he was debating whether he was going along with any of this. And Tim was just waiting to see who'd give first.

It was Summer. "The macaroni and cheese is almost ready," she said and this time, when she pulled away from Tim, he had no choice but to let her go.

He did want to eat, after all.

Dinner was interesting. Georgey kept looking at him, then Summer, then him again. Summer kept laughing in a high, tight way Tim took to mean she was nervous. And Tim—well, dinner was a hell of a lot better than anything he would've cooked for himself.

He couldn't quite figure out why Summer was so anxious, though. It wasn't as if Georgey didn't know people kissed. Knowing his mother, Tim wouldn't be surprised if the kid had walked in on a lot worse. And the kid had to have had girlfriends. He was attractive enough, in that dorky teenager way girls liked.

She kept up a steady stream of small talk, about the soccer game Georgey had coached and GED classes out of the college and whether Georgey should

Sarah M. Anderson

get his GED or if he should reenroll and finish high school traditionally. Georgey, for his part, kept his mouth shut and his eyes down. Odd.

Finally Summer seemed to run out of things to talk about. Which was fine, because they were done eating.

"Well!" she said, standing and grinning like a loon. "Georgey, why don't you start on the dishes while I check Tim's ribs."

Georgey smirked. "Is that what they're calling it these days?"

Summer shot tomato red and before he knew what he was doing, Tim leaned over and smacked the kid upside the back of the head. "Don't talk to your sister that way."

Summer gasped, her eyes wide with shock. "You two," she said in exasperation. Even though she was still bright red, she stood and pointed at Georgey. "You watch your attitude." The kid had the good sense to look at least a little cowered.

Then she swung that dangerous finger toward him. "And you. You can't keep smacking him around."

"Why not?" The moment he said it, Tim realized that was not the right thing. But honestly, he was a little confused. He tackled people, he shot people—he was, at this very moment, giving Nobody Bodine more-or-less a blank check to do all the same things.

"Because," Summer said, clearly flustered. "We are not allowed to touch the children under any circumstance. Period."

Tim couldn't help it. He cracked a grin. He glanced at Georgey and saw Georgey was trying not to laugh, too. "You know we're not in school, right?"

He was making this worse. Summer was so angry, he swore he could see steam start to come out of her ears. "Yes. Thank you. I'm aware I'm not at school. But there's still a code of conduct I believe must be upheld. And that includes no physical assaults on the children."

"He barely hit me," Georgey said, miraculously coming to Tim's defense when he could have easily piled on. "It's not a big deal."

"Of course it is," she shot back and stormed from the room.

"Get started on the dishes," Tim told Georgey. He forced himself to his feet and followed Summer.

Georgey might've made some noises of disapproval, but Tim ignored him. The kid had no room to talk anyway. "Summer?"

She was pacing in the bedroom, worrying the nail on her thumb. "I'm—I'm sorry," she said.

"For what?" He needed to tread carefully here.

"I overreacted, didn't I? I know I did." She stopped pacing and took some deep breaths that involved her hands pushing imaginary air in and out. "We're not allowed to touch the students," she said again, as if that explained everything.

"I picked up on that," he told her, easing himself down onto the bed. He left the door open on purpose because he suspected the fact that Georgey caught them kissing was at least sixty percent of the problem. "I don't beat kids, you know."

She looked stricken. "I didn't say you did. I'm just not used to the rules here. If I touched a student like that, I might've even been suspended from work. Violence is never the answer."

111

At that, Tim couldn't help but snort. He began to work the buttons on his uniform shirt. "That's a real pretty sentiment," he said, and he realized it came out sounding patronizing.

Now she was glaring at him. "You think I'm ridiculous."

It was not a question. "No, I don't. Like you said, you're not used to the rules around here. I'm sure in your world, people keep their hands to themselves and live in harmony. But in my world," he went on, wincing as he moved his arm to slide the shirt off, "violence is a way of life."

"You make it sound so…savage," she said in a whisper.

"Not the word I would've used," he said dryly. Then he hefted himself back to his feet. "How's this looking?"

As a subject change, it wasn't exactly subtle. But it worked. Summer's gaze dropped to his chest and he heard her suck in a little gasp of air. Then she stepped into him and reached out her hand. He tensed, but she didn't touch him, not right away. His chest was still wrapped and he wasn't exactly looking forward to having the bandage unwound.

"It's okay," he reassured her.

"I'm not sure it is," she said. "Turn around." Tim did as she asked and she undid the ends of the bandage and began winding it away from his skin.

As the gentle pressure that the elastic bandage had exerted against his chest was released, he winced as his muscles unclenched then stiffened in pain.

"It looks terrible," she told him, her fingertips lightly stroking over his bruised skin.

"It feels like hell," he agreed, then turned to face her. "There," he said lifting her chin and staring into her bright eyes. "I feel better already."

Embarrassment bloomed on her cheeks and her gaze cut to the doorway. "Georgey…"

Yeah, he guessed right. She was more embarrassed about being caught kissing than she was mad about him smacking the kid upside the head. He pointedly glanced toward the open door—and, thankfully, no one had his head poked through. "What about him?"

She shot him a dirty look. "We can't exactly do this with him around." Before he could ask what that meant, she quickly added, "Whatever *this* is."

"This," he said, settling his hands back on her hips and pulling her tight against him, "is two adults who are attracted to each other—right?"

She was tense in his arms, but only for a second before she melted. "Right," she said, but she didn't sound happy about it.

"Two consenting adults who don't have any other obligations, right?"

"Right," she said again, resting her head against his shoulder.

He was able to take a deep breath without too much pain, because she was there. "I don't see what the problem is."

She looked up at him and rolled her eyes. "This doesn't strike you as awkward at all?"

"The only awkward thing here is the fact that I'm exhausted and sore. If it weren't for that, I'd close that door and lay you down and pick right back up are we left off this afternoon."

His words had an immediate impact. Summer's

113

eyes widened and a flash of something that looked a hell of a lot like *want* crossed her face—before it was buried behind worry. "You can't be serious."

"Summer, the kid is seventeen. He knows what sex is."

He was not making this any better. "But he would know," she stammered out. "About us. About…you know."

Tim sighed again, which made his ribs pull. Maybe this wasn't a good idea. Yeah, he was attracted to her and yeah, she was attracted to him. But there was a whole hell of a lot more to a relationship than just sexual chemistry. The fact was, she might be too sweet and innocent to deal with a man like him. The gulf between their worlds might be too damned wide.

Still, what was she going to do when she got Georgey back to the big city? Was she going to spend the next year—or several years—not dating just because her brother might know she was kissing men?

She must've taken his sigh the wrong way because she got a worried look and said, "You take the bed. I'll sleep on the couch."

"What? No." He might not be the most chivalrous of men, but he wasn't about to let her sleep on that crappy couch. "You get the bed. Or," he added, cutting her off when her mouth opened to argue, "we can share the bed."

Her eyes got very wide. "We can't do that."

He cupped her face in his hands and stared down into her eyes. "Why don't you have a boyfriend?" Because that was the question that had been bothering him for a long time. "You're beautiful and caring and intelligent. You should have someone who'd miss you."

114

He could feel her blush as much as see it. The skin under his fingertips warmed. "I don't need a man just because I should have one."

He thought about that. "What about your friends? I know you told me you gave up your summer school job to stay out here a little while longer—won't your friends miss you?"

Something that looked like pain flashed in her eyes, then she pulled free of his grip so quickly he almost lost his balance. "I have friends," she said in the tight voice.

Something in him responded on a basic level— his gut instinct. The same gut instinct that told him Georgey wasn't hopeless.

She was lonely. He recognized it all too well.

"Who's going to miss you while you're here?"

Her spine stiffened. "I am not some pitiful spinster, you know," she snapped under her breath. "I have friends."

She hadn't answered the question. "You have your job," he said slowly, the truth dawning on him. "You have your students and your coworkers and your mom, right?"

She glared at him but she didn't answer.

"And you tell yourself that that's enough—but it's not. Not like this is." And before she could reply, he pulled her back into his arms and kissed her like he hadn't kissed a woman in so long, he wasn't sure he was doing it right.

In fact, he was pretty sure he was doing it wrong because her arms came up and she pushed him away. He let her, but he didn't let go of her.

"You do *not* know me," she breathed, her chest

115

rising and falling in anger. "You don't know me at all."

"I think I do—because that's how I feel, too."

"I don't—what?" She blinked up at him, momentarily stunned. "What are you talking about? This is where you belong."

"I know. This is my tribe and my people and my land—but I arrest so many of them and the ones who are left...I'm a stranger to them." He touched his forehead to hers. "And you—you *are* a stranger. But that's not how I feel when I'm with you."

"They would miss you," she insisted—but quietly. "I would miss you."

He breathed out slowly. "When you go back to the city, I'm going to miss you too." No, it didn't make any sense to him at all. He'd only known her for a matter of days. But there was something about her that called to him. "When you're around, I don't feel so alone."

And that? That was pitiful. That was weakness. And it wasn't the kind of weakness that could be prevented with a bulletproof vest.

He'd left himself open. Maybe it was the ribs. Maybe it was the exhaustion. Or maybe...maybe it was something else.

Maybe it was her.

She sighed, her warm breath caressing his skin. "Let me get you some more ice. And then," she added in what he thought of as her teacher voice, "you're going to lay on this bed and sleep."

He couldn't fight the grin that took hold of his mouth. "What about you?"

She stepped out of his arms and moved toward

the open door. When she reached it, she looked back at him and he saw the longing in her eyes. It was so strong he almost told her to come back and sleep with him tonight. Begged her to do just that.

"I can take care of myself," she told him.

And she walked away.

***

While she got the ice, she heard Tim in the bathroom. Amazingly, Georgey had the dishes almost done and set out on the drying rack. How long has she been in there with Tim? Summer's head pounded. Everything about this felt weird and wrong.

Except for the part where Tim held her and kissed her and told her that he wasn't as lonely when she was around.

"Is he okay?" Georgey asked quietly. "He looked like hell."

"I think so. He just needs to rest. I'm going to sleep out here on the couch tonight, if that's okay with you."

Georgey shrugged—typical teenage indifference.

She got the ice into the plastic grocery bag she'd borrowed from the childcare center. This way, it wouldn't leak as badly.

She wanted to hate Tim because he made her sound so damned pitiful. No boyfriend, and her work friends were all off having wild summer adventures of their own—without her. And her mother? Summer didn't even want to go there.

But she didn't think she could hate him. Because instead of throwing it in her face like her mother would've done or laughing it off like some of the guys in college had when she'd tried to explain the loneliness she'd felt, Tim understood.

She'd never been an Indian. Or a Native American or a Lakota or any of those things, except for that one time she'd come out to the reservation and stayed with her father for that week.

And there'd always been something…missing. Something that bothered her in the back of her mind every time her mother got going on her father and all his failings. Then she hadn't been all white, either. She'd been somewhere in between and, in all reality, in between was a pretty lonely place to be.

But it hadn't been something she'd been able to name until Tim Means had said, *We are all family.* Until she'd come to this place and found her brother.

Her head buzzing, she headed back to the bedroom. Tim had laid out towels on the bed again and was sitting on it, looking beat. He'd changed into a loose-fitting pair of gym shorts and right now, he looked almost nothing like the stern sheriff who'd found her lost in the grasslands.

But as she approached him, he hefted himself to his feet and lifted his arms as best he could so that she could wrap him again.

"Summer…" he said in a low voice.

She cut him off before he could say something that would make everything more confusing. "It's okay," she told him again.

But she should've known by now that a man like Tim Means would not be deterred. When she moved around to the front of his chest, he put his hands on her shoulders and held her still. "I'm tired and I'm sore and I'm sorry what I said hurt you. It wasn't my intention."

If it weren't for the part about him being tired and sore, she'd like to know exactly what his intentions were. Really, what did he want with her? Or even with Georgey? Because if this was just going to be a brief summer fling, well—that would be okay, wouldn't it?

But when a man stood in front of her and told her in all sincerity he was lonely and he'd miss her when she left, it didn't sound like a fling. She didn't know what, exactly, it sounded like—and that was the problem.

"Don't worry about it," she told him, tucking the ends of the bandage in and making sure the ice was over his bruise. "You need more than three hours of sleep. If you get up before six in the morning…"

She didn't actually have a threat she could make good on and he knew it. His lips quirked into a smile. "Yes?"

She swatted at his shoulder—the one on his good side. "You'll wake me up," she said in a dull voice.

"And nobody wants that," he grinned.

He looked like he wanted to say something else, so she leaned up on her toes and kissed him. "We'll talk more tomorrow—after you start feeling better."

She had a feeling that, if he were in better condition, he'd argue with her. But as it was, he nodded once and let her back him up to the bed. He winced as he leaned back, then she checked again to make sure the ice was in the right position before pulling the sheet over him.

He caught one of her hands in his and brought it to his mouth, where he kissed her palm. "Thank you," he said in a quiet voice, his eyes already shut.

She kissed him on the forehead. "I'll be here when you wake up."

Within seconds, his chest was rising and falling in even breaths. Summer couldn't help but notice he fell asleep with a smile on his face.

Chapter Nine

That night, Summer discovered exactly how uncomfortable the couch was. There was no good place to put her hips that didn't twist her back one way or the other. She finally decided laying on her side was the least-bad option.

Although Tim didn't have curtains on the window on the front of his house, it was still pitch black in the room. The only light came from the clock on the stove across the room in the kitchen. This was another thing completely different from her apartment back in Minneapolis. There, she had five blackout curtains to keep the light from the street lamps and cars from leaking into her bedroom. Here, there wasn't any of that. Tim's house was set off from the other houses she'd seen between here and the clinic or the police station. It was an almost physical representation of what he'd been talking about in the bedroom—being a part of the community but not really.

"The recliner is less lumpy, if you want to trade," Georgey said into the blackness.

Which, all things considered, was a downright thoughtful thing for a seventeen-year-old boy to say. "It's fine," she lied. After all, Georgey was a growing boy. Besides, she had no idea what Tim was going to have the kid doing tomorrow. He needed the rest.

121

But seeing as neither of them were asleep, Summer had some questions. "Georgey?"

"Yeah?"

"What do you want to do with the rest of your life?"

She heard the boy groan. "I don't know."

She propped herself up on her elbow and stared in his general direction, even though she couldn't see him. "Well, what did you want to be when you grew up?"

She heard the recliner shift and she imagined he was shrugging his shoulders. "Don't know," he repeated.

Boys. Either they thought they were going to be the next LeBron James or they didn't have a clue. "We need a plan," she told him.

"Why?"

"Why? Because if you don't have a plan—a goal to work for—then you're gonna wind up bumping along and that's when you get into trouble. You do stupid stuff like trying to break into a medical clinic instead of looking at the big picture. If you have a job, you know you'll be able to afford medicine for your grandma. Or your own car. Or your own apartment with a bed that doesn't suck like this couch does."

Georgey snorted. "I offered to trade," he reminded her.

Although he couldn't see it, she rolled her eyes. "That was literally the least important part of that entire statement."

"Well, I don't know," he said again, this time more firmly. "It's hard to plan for the future when you don't know how you're gonna eat tomorrow—or tonight. It's hard to work for a goal when you're not sure if you'll freeze to death because the electricity's been cut off again." His voice was louder and angrier. "It's hard to think big picture when the small picture is so huge you'll never get around it. *Never*."

There was so much hopelessness in his voice—in his life. She felt stupid again because she knew on some level what he said was true. After all, she'd seen it with her own students.

But she wasn't going to let him wallow in self-pity. "Well, you're going to start thinking big picture. I'm a big picture person and I'm more than happy to take care of you while we work on your big picture, but you're almost a man. You can't spend the rest of your life living with me."

He was quiet for a few moments. She wondered if he was going to pretend to have fallen asleep. Not that she was going to buy that.

"Did you always know what you wanted to be?" He sounded younger, more like a little brother than an angry teenager.

"Sort of. I wanted to be a cowgirl—and an Indian princess," she admitted. "I knew I was an Indian, but I only have a few memories of our dad before he and Mom got divorced. Mostly, I just remember coming back for a pow wow when I was twelve and you weren't quite three yet." She swallowed. "Do you remember that? We played together. I was…" She took a deep breath. "I was so glad to have a little brother."

The silence filled the room. "I don't remember," he finally said, his voice barely a whisper. "I wish I did, though. If I'd known…"

She understood. How would things have been different if she'd kept her promise to her father before now? If Georgey had known he could've called her before he'd gotten arrested?

She cleared her throat, which was suspiciously tight. "To answer your question, I always liked school."

Georgey snorted. "Weirdo."

She grinned. "I didn't say it was normal. But I did. I liked school and I liked my teachers and I did well, so it seemed like the most logical choice. I don't know anything about horses and cows." Or about being an Indian. But she pulled her thoughts away from that direction. "Don't get me wrong—by the end of the school year, I'm just as tired of school as everyone else. Right now, I never want to read *Romeo and Juliet* again."

"Is that a book?"

She sat all the way up at that. "It's a play," she said in a careful tone. "By William Shakespeare?" Surely he had heard of Shakespeare. Hadn't everyone?

"You read a play in class?" He sounded as careful as she felt.

She realized he was admitting something to her, in his way. "Georgey, when did you drop out?"

Silence.

This was not good. "Georgey?" Because she assumed he dropped out—well, if he was seventeen, hadn't he at least made it to tenth grade?

"I'm not stupid," he whispered in a fierce voice.

"I don't believe you are," she said honestly.

"It's just that the words—I don't think they look right. I mean, the letters…" He swallowed so loudly she could hear it, even in the darkness. "I don't read.

They said it was because I was stupid and lazy but if they tell me what's on the page, I can remember."

"They?"

"My teachers," he said in a defeated voice. "I got held back a couple times and they said I'd have to take eighth grade again…"

Oh, God. He hadn't even made it past eighth grade. She had been operating under the assumption he only needed a year or two at most—that he could finish up at school with her or get his GED.

"Did any of them ever say the word dyslexia?" she asked gently. She was no expert on learning disabilities but she had enough students who had dyslexia on their IEPs.

"I don't know. Maybe. My fifth grade teacher was nice."

Summer dropped her head into her hands and tried to think. In her school district, there were special education teachers who were experts in dealing with learning disabilities and dyslexia. There were workarounds—audio recordings of lectures, verbal tests, exercises to help train their brains to make sense of the letters.

"Did they ever put you in a special class?"

"No," he said, as if that idea were an affront to his personal pride.

This was terrible—and suddenly, everything made sense. This was the final piece to the puzzle, one she hadn't known was missing.

Georgey was dyslexic. Because the schools around here were so crappy, no one had even known, except for maybe one teacher back in fifth grade. Instead the poor kid had been completely on his own.

125

This was not what she had signed up for. It was, however, something she was at least somewhat qualified to deal with.

There was only one problem. Even if she got Georgey correctly diagnosed, there was no way in hell the seventeen-year-old boy was going to go back to the eighth grade. And she couldn't afford to quit her job and homeschool him.

"Am I…" He sounded scared and she wasn't sure why until he finished the sentence. "Am I in trouble?"

"Good Lord, no. I think you're dyslexic, though. Your brain flips some letters and numbers around and it makes it hard to process what you're seeing. It doesn't mean you're stupid," she hurried to add. "It just means you have to learn in a different way—and it sounds like you never had a teacher who knew how to help you do that."

He snorted again. "I don't think I've ever had a teacher who knew anything about anything." He sighed. "That fifth grade teacher… She wanted me to go to the Catholic school. She said she had friends there who could help me better than she could. But that cost money and Mom wouldn't pay it and Grandma couldn't." He huffed. "And Dad was dead. I barely remember him."

Everyone had failed this kid. She didn't necessarily want to lump her father in with that, but he had gone and died ten years ago. Georgey's mom hadn't even tried. His grandma had done her best, but there was only so much one old woman in poor health with no money could do, apparently. Every other teacher he'd ever had and every other adult in his life had let him down. Even her, because she hadn't kept an eye on her brother for all those years.

"We don't have any money," came Georgey's quiet voice out of the darkness again. "And Grandma can't see anymore and I thought that if I took her in to the clinic, they'd make me try to read something or sign something and I can't do it. So I thought I'd just take what I needed because I didn't want them to tell me I was stupid again. I didn't want to—I didn't see how I had a choice."

Until Tim came along. Tim, who could have easily given up on this kid and shunted him down the system into juvvie or foster care. Instead, he tracked Summer down and put Georgey to work righting his wrongs.

"Anyone who calls you stupid is an idiot," she told him. "This is going to take a little work for me to figure out, though." Wasn't *that* the understatement of the year. "In the meantime, I want you to start thinking about what you want to do for the rest of your life. You let me worry about food and a place to sleep and your education for now."

"Okay." He sounded relieved and she wondered if he'd been waiting for her to blow up at the news that he could barely read. Had he spent the last several days waiting for her to abandon him?

The poor kid. "Get some sleep," she told him, lying back down on the couch of doom. "You've got a big day tomorrow."

"Yeah, right." Then, "Are you sure you don't want the recliner?"

"I'm sure."

She lay there for a long time, listening as Georgey's breath evened out. Obviously the local school system couldn't handle him. But this wasn't the sort of thing she could put off until the next school year. Georgey was already so far behind.

She had only one other place to check. The local community college.

***

Summer Collins was not a morning person. Tim got up, showered, got the coffee perking and shook Georgey awake—and she slept through the whole thing.

Tim got some coffee into the kid then carried a cup over to her. As best he could, he crouched down beside her. "Summer."

"Mmph," was the response he got.

"We're leaving," he told her and he couldn't help but brush a few loose strands of her light brown hair off her face. His fingers curled around her cheek on their own. "I saved you a cup of coffee."

"Coffee?" One of her eyelids managed to prop itself open at half-mast. "Oh," she exhaled. "Hi."

He grinned down at her. "Good morning. Is there anything you need before we go?"

His hand was still cupping her cheek, his thumb stroking over her freckles. Her hand snaked up to the back of his neck and pulled him down. Then she was kissing him and he wanted nothing more than to let her, but Georgey was behind him, apparently choking on his coffee.

So Tim pulled away—not because he wanted to, but because he knew she would be embarrassed when she woke up enough to realize she'd kissed him in front of the kid. "If you need anything," he told her, "call the police station."

128

She blinked at him a couple times, her eyelids almost moving in unison—but not quite. He saw the moment she actually woke up. "Oh! Tim! Are you okay?"

"I'm better," he reassured her. It wasn't a lie. He'd gotten close to ten hours of solid sleep. He was still sore as hell and the bruise had turned a dull, angry purple on his ribs. But his mind felt clearer than it had for a couple days and, assuming no one declared war on the rez within the next twenty-four hours, he just might survive. "You going to be okay today?"

She sat up and gratefully accepted the cup of coffee he held out for her. "Where's the nearest grocery store? And how do I get to that college you were telling me about?"

"There's a convenience store not too far away if you need something—otherwise the nearest grocery store is in Wall, but it's kind of small. The kind you're used to, you've got to go to Rapid City. The college is in the other direction, about an hour away."

She took a long drink of the coffee. "Okay," she said. "Is there a place on this reservation with an Internet connection?"

"There'd be one at the college. I don't think Dr. Mitchell has gotten the clinic wired yet, but you can always ask." A lock of her hair had fallen back in her face and he brushed it away. "We'll see you tonight, okay?"

She yawned. "Okay."

Reluctantly Tim backed away from her. He looked at Georgey and nodded toward the door. The kid scowled, but he followed.

Tim didn't exactly feel up to making small talk, so they drove in silence. He had the feeling the kid had things he wanted to say, so he was just going to let Georgey say them in his own time.

Finally, the kid broke. "So are you two dating or what?"

Tim rolled his eyes at the attitude loaded into every single syllable of that question. "And it's your business...why?"

Georgey scoffed. "Because she's my sister?"

Tim slid a hard look at the boy. "Seems to me it hasn't been two weeks since you were in a cell telling me you didn't have any family."

Georgey scowled back. "Well I do. You got a problem with that?"

Obviously the kid was looking for a fight. The thing was, Tim wasn't in the mood to be anyone's punching bag. "No. Do you?"

"Asshole."

"For a kid who owes me some physical labor, you sure got a mouth on you today."

"I don't want to see her hurt. She's not like other people around here. She's different."

"You're not telling me something I don't already know." It was good he was worried about her, Tim decided. If the kid was worried, that meant he cared. And if he cared, that meant he hadn't given up yet. "What did you guys talk about last night, after I went to sleep?" Tim had awoken briefly a couple times and heard low voices coming from the living room. But he'd been too tired to wake up enough to understand what they were saying.

Georgey didn't answer right away and Tim let the silence stretch. Finally, the kid said, "Have you ever heard of... dis-lex-ee-a?"

"Sure, dyslexia. It's when you can't read the letters and words right, right?"

"That's what she says. She thinks maybe that's what's wrong with me."

Tim turned to look at the boy. He knew Georgey had dropped out of school—but he thought it was the same reason everyone else on this rez always dropped out of school.

What was the point? They weren't going to go to college and they weren't going to get good jobs and they didn't have any hope for the future. Instead they gave up and joined gangs and got drunk and high and died way too early. *So* many of them died way too early.

"I didn't think there was anything wrong with you," he said in a neutral voice because it seemed obvious, from the way that the kid was blushing, he was embarrassed by this admission.

"Well, there is. I can't read. And she's this teacher and she said she was gonna take me back to the city and put me in high school and..." Georgey's voice caught. "And I can't read and everybody's going to make fun of me and I'll be stuck there."

What the hell was Tim supposed to do with that? No clue. He'd assumed the kid could at least read. "But she's going to take care of you," he said, trying to find the right words to reassure Georgey.

"For a little while, anyway. That was the other thing she asked me last night. What do I want to be when I grow up? Because I can't stay with her forever." He still sounded mad at the world, but this time Tim saw the truth of it. He was mad, all right—but he was also scared shitless.

131

Sarah M. Anderson

Because what could a kid who couldn't read grow up to be?

Tim had a feeling that at this point, Summer would've done something comforting, like haul the kid into a hug and tell him it was going to be all right. She was like that.

Tim wasn't. "What did you tell her?"

"I don't know."

Tim exhaled dramatically. "Well, when you're done feeling sorry for yourself, you let me know."

Georgey bristled, and Tim bit down on his inner cheek to keep from smiling. "I am *not* feeling sorry for myself."

"You're not? That's what it sounds like to me. So reading is hard. Yeah, dyslexia sucks but I got news for you, kid—life is hard. We all get handed a short stick every now and again. You can either sit around feeling sorry for yourself or you can do something about it. Summer can help solve the problem and she's going to take care of you so you're not on your own. But you've got to do your part, too. It's up to you."

He waited for Georgey to respond, but before the boy could come up with anything that probably wasn't a cuss word, Tim's CB radio crackled to life. "Tell me you're on your way," Jack asked.

Dammit. He hadn't even made it to work this morning before it all went to hell in a handbasket. He picked up the CB mic and said, "What?"

"Clarence called—he's got a kid with a gunshot wound at the clinic. Can you get there or do I need to take this?"

Tim mentally translated that. He'd bet dimes to dollars Jack was sitting in his police car in the

132

driveway of his trailer, probably without a shirt on, hoping like hell he'd be able to get a couple more hours of sleep. "I got this. I'll call you at home if I need you."

"Yep."

Tim pulled a U-turn in the middle of the road and gunned it toward the clinic. He glanced over at Georgey and saw he was pale. He knew what the kid was thinking, too—which one of his friends had been shot?

***

It was Shorty. The moment Tim got the door to the clinic opened, he could hear the kid whimpering. Tim glanced back at Georgey, who was still pale. But he set his jaw into a grim line and wasn't backing down.

Tara, the receptionist, looked up at them and sighed in relief. "Oh, thank God. Shorty won't tell us anything—he won't stop moaning, either. He's freaking the other patients out."

"I take it he's not on the verge of death?" Tim said. Tara was not known for her warm and fuzzy attitude.

She jerked her chin toward the back of the room, where Shorty was indeed moaning behind a curtain. "No, he's not dying. He just thinks he is. Go on back."

"Let me handle this," Tim said in a quiet voice. He didn't know if Georgey was going to pass out or throw up—but Nobody Bodine had said Georgey needed to be scared and there was nothing like seeing a friend with a hole in his body to do the scaring. With

133

any luck, this would ensure both Shorty and Georgey stayed on the straight and narrow from here on out.

"Clarence?"

The big man's head popped through the curtain. He saw Tim and grinned. "Try not to laugh," he whispered.

Tim shot him a funny look. In his experience, gunshot wounds weren't laughing matters. "I've got Georgey with me today," he said, acting as if Georgey were here on purpose instead of accidentally along for the ride.

"That's fine. The kid is scared. Maybe Georgey will calm him down." Clarence parted the curtain and Tim and Georgey stepped through.

Tim immediately had to bite his lip to keep from laughing. Because poor Shorty's bare ass was up in the air. He had been shot in the butt.

Tim glanced back at Georgey, whose eyes had gotten big. He wasn't giggling and he hadn't passed out, so this counted as a win. "Shorty, I thought when I let you go a couple days ago, you were going to stay out of trouble."

At the sound of his voice, Shorty jerked—then moaned again. "What are you doing here?" he got out through clenched teeth.

"You're not going to believe this, but it's illegal to shoot a kid on my rez. Even if that kid is a dumbass sometimes." Tim walked around to the head of the bed where he was able to *not* look Shorty in the butt. "You're smarter than this, kid. You're mixed up with the Killerz and I'm hauling your ass out of gunfights and when I'm not, you're getting it shot. Who did this?"

Shorty closed his eyes and turned his head to the side. He didn't moan, so there was that.

Georgey stood back by Clarence, looking at Shorty's wound. "That's not a very big hole," Georgey observed.

Shorty jumped again, which led to more moaning. But then he said, "Georgey? What are you doing here?"

Tim didn't rush into the silence. At no point was "doing community service" a cool thing to say to your friends, and he was curious to see what Georgey would come up with.

Georgey glanced that Tim, then looked back down at Shorty's butt. "I'm doing a ride-along with the sheriff today. I'm thinking about becoming a cop when I get my GED."

That was the first Tim had heard about it, but he wasn't about to contradict the kid. Especially because it was a decent idea.

"Does it hurt?" Georgey asked, turning his attention back to the gunshot wound.

"No," Shorty lied.

Both Clarence and Tim snorted. Clarence said, "Given the size of the hole, I'm thinking this was rat shot or a pellet gun. Doesn't appear to have hit any major blood vessels."

Tim walked back around and looked at the hole. It was small—maybe a .13? That'd be rat shot for sure. "How deep?" Tim asked.

"One sec." Then he said to Shorty, "If it doesn't hurt yet, it's about to start." Clarence jabbed in a needle—painkillers, probably—and began to dig the bullet out. Shorty made a noise that sounded like a howl that he refused to let out.

Tim was never one to let a good interrogation moment pass by unused. He went back to look Shorty in the face. It was a better deal anyway. "You didn't shoot yourself in the butt," he said, watching tears gather in the corner of Shorty's eyes. He glanced over at Georgey, who was still pale but staring in fascination at what Clarence was doing. "So that leaves me with one of two conclusions. Either someone shot you to punish you and you're afraid to roll on them, or this was a prank gone horribly wrong and you don't want to roll on your friends. Which is it?"

"Go to hell," Shorty got out through gritted teeth.

"Where'd you learn how to do that?" Georgey said, sounding fascinated.

"The Navy, kid. Tim was in the Army and Jack—well, he's not allowed to tell us where he was, but I wouldn't piss him off if I were you." Clarence held up a pair of long tweezers with a small metal lump in them. "Rat shot," he said with great finality. "Only about two inches in."

"So, fifteen to twenty feet away?" Interesting. Rat shot wasn't as common these days. He'd be willing to bet there were only a few people on this rez that had a decent supply of it. If it'd been a pellet, it might have been impossible to trace. But rat shot made his job that much easier.

"That be my guess—but you're the artillery expert. I just patch them up." Clarence dropped the slug into a pan and began to disinfect the wound. Shorty stiffened in pain. "If you're thinking about being a cop, you wouldn't do bad to join the military," he told Georgey in a casual voice. "Try not to scream," he added.

Shorty screamed anyway and then Clarence was bandaging him up and putting a sheet over his butt. Still Shorty hadn't said anything about who'd shot him.

Georgey came around to Shorty's head. "Your ass looks terrible, man. You're not going to be able to sit down for a month."

"Fuck off," Shorty bit out.

Georgey shifted from one foot to the other and Tim realized how young he still looked—how young they both did. Just kids.

"Are you gonna be okay?" Georgey asked.

"What do you care? We don't hang out since you dropped out."

"You're my friend," Georgey said as if that weren't some obvious fact. "I'd never shoot you. And I hope you wouldn't shoot me, either. This is just your butt, man—but what if next time, it's not?"

Tim leaned back and gave Georgey room to work. Shorty wouldn't tell Tim anything because he was a cop—but he might open up to his friend. Maybe.

Shorty didn't say anything yet, but Tim could tell he was trying not to cry.

"Yeah, well," he said, his voice ragged, "you're not Levi, are you?"

"Levi shot you? Why would he do that?" Georgey sounded genuinely confused by this, but Tim had a few ideas.

Shorty had been the first one to talk to Tim after he busted up the gang fight. He'd been the first one Tim sent home. If someone were paranoid, he might think Shorty was the first person to turn on him. And if Levi was dealing with Los Perros, he was bound to be nothing if not paranoid.

137

Dammit. The fact that Levi made bail was bad enough. But now this? Firing warning shots into boys?

Nope. Not on his rez.

Tim and Clarence looked at each other and Tim nodded. Clarence slipped out through the curtain to get an evidence bag for the bullet.

"You wouldn't understand," Shorty said miserably.

Georgey crouched down so he could look Shorty in the eye. "Dude, it doesn't have to be like this."

Shorty closed his eyes and turned his head away.

Georgey stood up straight and put his hands on his hips, looking disgusted. "Fine, be that way. But I'm still your friend." He stormed out from the curtains.

Tim waited.

"You gonna tell my mom?" Shorty finally said in a quiet voice.

Tim snorted. "You think you're going to be able to hide the fact you can't sit down from her?" At least Shorty's mom still cared. She couldn't keep up with her kids, but she tried and that counted for a lot. "We can't keep doing this, boy. This is the second time in three days I've seen you. Do you know where we go from here?"

"Fuck off," Shorty replied.

It took a lot to get under Tim's skin but this kid was putting in the extra effort. "Here's how this goes. The next time I see you, you'll either be dead or I'll lock you in a cell. This isn't a question. This is a fact. Levi might shoot you in the face—and not with some dinky little rat shot—because he wants to make an example out of you. That's if your luck runs out. Or you'll do something stupid to prove to him that you're still his little errand boy and I'll bust what's left of your ass down to brass tacks so fast you won't have time to tell anyone to fuck off. Do I make myself clear? And if I have to lock you in a cell to keep you safe, I will."

He realized he was shouting but here he was again, struggling to keep another kid alive and out of jail and this time, he was losing the battle. He'd have thought nearly getting his head blown off in a turf war then being scared shitless by Nobody would have put the fear of God into Shorty—but no. He'd gone right back to Levi—and paid the price.

"Anyone else around when he shot you?" If there were other witnesses willing to put the gun in Levi's hands, retaliation would be harder to successfully pull off.

"No," came the weak reply.

Yup. Paranoia in action. "I'm going to call your mom—assuming Tara hasn't done so already. You're going to lay low for the rest of this damn summer."

"No!" Shorty was openly crying now.

Tim waited, letting the silence stretch.

"He said if I talked to you again, he'd kill me." The kid looked up at him, eyes wide with terror. "He thinks I told you about the guns."

Tim cursed silently. Shorty hadn't—but Georgey had. Crap. What Tim needed was a plan. He couldn't have Levi running around his rez—but he wasn't about to dangle a terrified fifteen-year-old boy with a flesh wound as bait.

He had to get Shorty off this rez without anyone knowing about it. Which really only left him with one option.

The kid was not going to like this.

He crouched down close to Shorty's ear, just in case anyone was listening. "I'm going to call your mom and you're going to go home and pack a bag and wait," Tim told him. "Nobody will come get you and he'll get you off this rez."

"What?" Shorty yelped.

Tim smacked the kid on the shoulder. "Shut up, Shorty. I'm trying to save your damn life. Your grandma—she still lives over on Rosebud?" The kid nodded, biting his lip. "You're going to stay with her for the rest of the summer—no arguments. If I find you on the White Sandy, I'll arrest you."

"But my sister..." he whimpered. "Gramma doesn't have that much money..."

Goddamnit all to hell. It would be hard enough for the older woman to feed one extra mouth—two would be impossible. Tim squeezed his eyes shut. If Levi was okay with shooting his own gopher, he might just take a little girl as insurance.

Thankfully, Tim had an option. "I have a place I can put her for the summer—not with you," he added. The Last Hope ranch butted up against the far western edge of the White Sandy and was run by Sam Kenady, the granddaughter of one of Tim's grandmother's oldest friends. Sam hadn't grown up on the rez, but she took in strays and lost souls—as long as they were women. No men were allowed on the Last Hope ranch. Sam would take in a twelve-year-old girl for the summer, as long as the kid was willing to work.

"But if I send you to your grandmother's, you have to help out. She's not your maid, got it? And if you get in trouble again, I won't protect you. Understood?"

140

He thought the boy nodded, which was good enough. Tim left him quietly crying in his little curtained room. God, he hated this. He hated when his own people declared war on their kids. Levi was becoming a problem that needed a solution.

Levi was a problem because Dwayne was in prison. If Tim locked Levi up, someone else would rush into the void. It'd never end, this vicious circle of violence he was stuck in. All he could do was try to hold back the chaos, working long hours and hoping that when—not if—he got shot, it hit him in the vest and just bruised him. And all he could do was take it, take the simmering hatred and the deaths and the suffering—and he'd take it alone. This was his burden, his cross to bear.

Then he saw Georgey waiting for him, a small plastic baggie with a bullet in his hand. And he remembered the kid said maybe he wanted to be a cop—after he got his GED. And he remembered Summer was at his place, that she'd wrapped his ribs and made him dinner and kissed him this morning before she'd been awake enough to realize it, simply because she was glad to see him. And he was going back home to her tonight, him and Georgey.

And he thought *maybe*...

It was still his burden, but maybe he could carry it just a little bit longer.

Chapter Ten

The problem with the reservation, Summer decided, was it was in the middle of nowhere. She knew that, of course—she'd already been lost on it once. But driving an hour to get to the community college, then driving almost another two and a half hours to get to a grocery store in Rapid City and driving back to Tim's place to put the groceries away was basically her day. Why was a convenience store the only place to get groceries on this whole reservation? For Pete's sake. What did the people who couldn't drive to Wall or Rapid City do for food?

But the good news was the community college was delighted to have a certified teacher pick up a few GED classes and tutor students who needed help with English. Not for a lot of money—minimum wage. But still, it was some money and her hours would be flexible. The kind of flexible where she could pretty much show up and leave whenever she wanted.

Plus she could bring Georgey with her whenever she wanted. So as soon as Tim got done making him fulfill his community service, such as it was, she could spend the rest of the summer working with Georgey on his reading. A GED might be out of reach right now, but if she could at least get him tested into a high-school level when they got back to Minneapolis…

It was strange how not-exciting the thought of going back felt.

There was one staff member at the college who had worked with dyslexic students before, but Summer was essentially on her own here. She'd logged into the college's wifi and done some research. Her instincts had been mostly correct—audio books, lectures instead of assigned readings, that sort of thing.

But something else she'd found on a website mentioned using magazines and graphic novels—lots of pictures, smaller groups of words—to work on reading. Even comic strips could be useful. The smaller texts were less overwhelming, apparently. While she had a functioning connection, she'd downloaded some audio books to her phone—the entire Harry Potter series and the Percy Jackson series for starters. Boys in her classes read those—plus, Percy Jackson had dyslexia. Perfect.

Thus armed with knowledge and something that felt like a plan, Summer promised she'd be back the next day. She'd then driven to Rapid City to shop at a Supermart.

Tim did not have an abundance of food—certainly not enough for three people, especially when one of those three was an underfed teenaged boy. Last night's dinner had been scraping the very bottom of his pantry. She knew Tim didn't expect her to cook and do the shopping, but she felt like it was the least she could do, considering how far out of his way he'd gone to take in Georgey and make room for her.

The odd thing was, it had almost nothing to do with him kissing her.

Almost.

He'd left before she really woken up this

morning. She was pretty sure she'd kissed him and coffee had been involved, but beyond that?

She had all that time in the car today to think over what he'd said last night.

Who, back in Minneapolis, was missing her right now? And when she went back to that life, would it be enough?

A part of her was 100% certain it was. She was Summer Collins. She was a teacher. She had friends and a life. Sure, she was still establishing herself. She had a small—no, scratch that—*cozy* apartment. And no, she didn't have a big social circle. But she wasn't the kind of person who needed one. She got all her peopling done at school and was perfectly happy to go home and enjoy the peace and quiet. So no, Tim didn't know her at all.

Except...

She didn't need a bunch of people to miss her. But one or two might be nice.

Which was why, before she did her shopping, she found herself in the parking lot of Supermart, doing the very last thing she wanted to do.

She called her mother.

"Where are you?" her mother snapped before Summer could even say *hi*. Which was not the best start to the conversation.

"Rapid City. South Dakota," she added, although she didn't know why. Her mother was many things, but clueless about basic geography wasn't one of them.

There was a tense pause. "I can't help but realize that's on the far side of the state. Not closer to Minnesota." It sounded like her mother was grinding her teeth.

Summer grimaced and ignored the guilt trip. "There's no reception on the reservation, Mom. I came into town to get some groceries and wanted to check in with you. How are you? Is everything okay?"

"You're not coming home?" Each word was an accusation.

"Of course I'm coming home," she protested, trying to figure out how to get out of this call and knowing full well it was her own damned fault she was having this conversation in the first place. Of course, if she hadn't checked in, her mother would be furious too. Basically there was no way Summer could win, so she might as well take her lumps now. "But I'm going to be out here for a few more weeks. I got a part-time job," she offered weakly.

"You're staying out there?" Each word was a dagger tipped with the most dangerous poison known to womankind—guilt. "Out there with...*them*?"

"Mom..."

"Don't you 'Mom' me, young lady. This is completely unacceptable. I've spent years shielding you from the poor choices your father made—years, I tell you."

"Poor choices? Mom, he didn't choose to be Lakota."

Linda Collins physically hissed at the word, as if Summer had said *fuck off* instead of the proper name of her tribe. "Those people are nothing but drunks."

She thought of Tim, of Georgey and Jack and Clarence and Tammy and even Nobody, that shadowy guy. Not a drunk among them.

In fact, if it weren't been for the small matter of the gang war, Summer hadn't seen anything unusual,

145

except more poverty than she was comfortable with. "They're just people, Mom. Like you and me."

Her mother gasped in true horror.

Why had Summer said that? Why was she pushing the issue? All she'd needed to do was call and check in and let her mother lecture her a little bit, then get on with her day. She had a huge shopping list and a long drive home and...

Except it wasn't home, not hers. It was Tim's home. She was just a guest.

"This is unacceptable, Summer. Just completely unacceptable. I raised you better than this."

Something in her mind snapped. "And how was that? White? You cut me off from half my culture!"

A stunned silence gripped both of them. What the hell had she just said? Summer mentally replayed the accusation—that was the only thing she could call it—but it'd just appeared out of nowhere.

It was also the unfortunate truth. Her mother had cut her father out of her life, and with him, everything that made her a Lakota. Including her brother.

And Summer had just...let her. Tim had been right. She was missing something and she'd found it on a windswept prairie.

"You are not one of them," her mother said in a dangerously low voice. "And I can't believe you would throw away everything I've done to protect you..."

"Well, it's been nice chatting," Summer heard herself say, as if she were very far away from herself. "But I've got errands to run. I'll let you know when I'm back in Minneapolis, okay? Take care. Love you, Mom."

Before her mother could say anything else, Summer hung up. She sat there for long minutes, staring at her phone. She half thought her mom might call her back, but she didn't and Summer didn't hit redial, either.

Is that what her mother told herself? That she was protecting Summer from—from what? From some harsh reality, where Linda Collins had married Leonard Two Elks, then changed her mind? From knowing half her own family? From…

From having someone who would miss her when she was gone?

Well, one thing was for certain.

She was *done* being shielded.

***

By the time Tim pulled up in front of this house, it was past six and he was pretty sure he hadn't fed Georgey lunch. Nothing today had gone like it was supposed to. What should have been a quiet day at the station, getting caught up on paperwork while Georgey scrubbed the whole place, had turned into an all-day affair of tracking down people and making plans and back-up plans and trying to find Levi and failing.

For better or worse, Tim had given Georgey a true ride-along. In addition to trying to get Shorty taking care of, Tim had also gone out on three other calls. Some idiot had tried to stick up the Kum N' Go gas station on the north edge of the rez, but the clerk held a shotgun on the would-be robber until Tim rolled in and arrested the guy—some white guy from off the rez, which meant more paperwork and more headaches.

There'd been a domestic battery call, with a wife who insisted she didn't want to press charges—or be taken to the Clinic to have her black eyes checked out. And there had been a report of drag racing—although no one had been at the site of the race by the time Tim and Georgey got there.

All in all, it had been one hell of a busy day. Tim was hungry, he was tired and he hurt. That was normal. He could deal with it if that was all. But it wasn't.

"… go with you tomorrow?" Georgey was saying excitedly as he put his shoulder to the door.

"We'll see," Tim said, then the smell of something wonderful hit him—fried chicken.

He absolutely did not expect Summer Collins to cook for him. And he was equally sure he didn't have any chicken. But God, after the day he had? Almost twelve solid hours of hauling Georgey around and trying to keep the peace on this rez? And to know when he came home, not only would she be here, but she'd do something simply wonderful, like making dinner?

Summer Collins was too good to be true. It was heaven.

"Summer!" Georgey said, bursting into the house before Tim could string together two coherent thoughts. "It was so cool! I'm gonna be a cop when I grow up!"

Summer turned from where was frying chicken at the stove. "Is that so?" she said in what Tim considered to be a very calm voice.

"Yeah! I rode along with Tim all day today—it was *so* cool. Shorty got shot in the butt then we tried to find Levi and then we—"

"Zip it, kid." Tim shot Georgey a look. "Some of

148

that stuff is confidential, remember?" Because that had been the deal.

Georgey had to keep his mouth shut about the plan for Shorty. If anyone else knew where Shorty was going and how he was going to get there, the whole thing would be pointless. So far, the only people who knew were Tim, Shorty, Georgey, Nobody, Clarence and Jack. Tim wanted to keep it that way.

"Right, right." Georgey started hopping from foot to foot, which made him look all of twelve. Still, it was nice to see him excited about something

"Dinner is almost ready," Summer said in a gentle voice. Or maybe that was just a normal voice. Maybe she just sounded gentler than anyone else had all day long. "Georgey, go wash up. And after dinner, I have some things for you."

Georgey looked like he might want to argue with this, but then he said, "Did you buy me...presents?"

Summer winked. Winked! "I might have. Scoot." She lifted out another piece of fried chicken and put it on a plate. Georgey's mouth went slack and Tim was pretty sure he was drooling. He felt even worse because he definitely hadn't made sure the kid ate lunch today.

Once the bathroom door clicked, Tim was able to take a deep breath. "You don't have to make me dinner."

She turned the stove off. "I know. Don't get used to it. I'll be putting in some hours at the community college. And I'll be able to take Georgey with me, so you won't have to babysit him all day."

"He was fine," Tim said. He realized Summer was walking toward him and he felt that certainty all over again.

149

He could love her.

He would miss her when she left—he didn't want her to go. Right now, he had no idea how to make her stay, either.

"How are you?" She touched her hand to his chest.

"Better." He pulled her in to him and kissed her, because he wanted to, because it felt like the most natural thing in the world.

He lost track of time—of everything. Everything but the way she sighed into him and the way her body molded to his. He kissed her harder, tracing the seam of her lips with his tongue and groaning with satisfaction when she opened for him.

No one on this rez was ever glad to see him. Except for Summer Collins.

"Tim…" she sighed into him. In his ears, it sounded like a plea for something else. Something *more*.

He cupped her face and stared down at her. Something was different about her. "Are you okay?"

She laughed at that. "Better," she breathed, leaning up on her tiptoes to brush her lips against his again. "I think I'm better."

Tim groaned as she pulled his hat from his head and sank her fingers into his hair. This had to be a dream. There simply wasn't any other explanation for the turn his life had taken this week. A beautiful woman waiting for him at the end of a long day? Homemade food? Her body pressing against his, her mouth exploring his?

"Oh, gross."

Tim winced as Georgey waltzed back into the

room. He'd just needed another minute. Or twenty. She'd been right about one thing last night—how were they supposed to do this with an opinionated teenage male in the house?

But instead of another editorial comment, Georgey walked over to the plate of cooling chicken and said, "Summer, are you gonna cook like this all the time when I live with you? Because if so, maybe it won't be so bad. What's this?"

The thing was, she hadn't jerked herself out of Tim's arms when Georgey came back in to the room. Instead, she leaned her head on his chest and just held him. "Mashed potatoes," she said, glancing over her shoulder to see Georgey holding up the bowl of spuds. "Haven't you ever had mashed potatoes before?"

"Well, yeah—but these are yellowish with green things in them."

"Cheesy mashed potatoes with chives. They're good, trust me." She looked up at Tim. "I want to hear all about your day—the parts you can tell me," she added before she turned back to the table.

All he could do was stand there in stunned silence. Was it wrong to want this? Was it wrong to want her?

No. No, it wasn't.

He wanted her. It was brilliant in its simplicity.

Now he just had to figure out how to hold onto her, even for a little while.

He needed to call in a favor.

Chapter Eleven

Morning, Jack."

Jack stared blearily at Tim. He leaned against the door to his trailer, bare-chested and looking like he'd been run over by a semi-truck. "Do you have any idea what time it is?"

"Ten in the morning," Tim replied. He'd been up for hours, but he didn't dare wait any longer before he talked to Jack. And this wasn't the sort of conversation he wanted to have over the phone. "I need a favor."

"Oh, this is going to be rich." Jack spun on his heel, leaving the door open. Tim took that as an invitation and followed the man inside. Jack basically lived in an RV, but had somehow managed to run water, electricity, and sewer to it. It was a newer vehicle, so everything was neat and clean.

"Nice place," he said. Trailers like this cost money. What was it Clarence had told Georgey? It was better not to ask about Jack.

So Tim didn't.

"Coffee?" Jack asked, sounding resigned to being awake. "Or are you going to insist on proper tea?"

"Coffee is fine, man." Tim sat down at one of the chairs at the narrow dining table. "Are you getting any sleep?"

Jack snorted. "No, I'm entertaining visitors. What do you want, Tim? I know this isn't about the job."

Tim winced. He got on well with Jack, better than he did with most people. They functioned well as a unit. But they weren't what he would call buddies. "It is, sort of. I need you to take Georgey on a ride-along, show him the night shift. He thinks he might want to be a cop after he helped Clarence dig rat shot out of Shorty's ass."

Jack froze for a moment, his hand halfway to the coffee maker. "Man," he said slowly. "We need to hire a third guy, but are you serious? That punk kid? He never even made it through high school, as far as I can tell."

Yeah, that was a problem. They did need another deputy—two would be better. They were relying too much on Nobody being an unofficial deputy and sooner or later, he was going to kill someone. "The kid's dyslexic. I don't think anyone realized. But his sister is going to get him up to speed, help him get his GED. And if that happens, we can throw him into the Army for a few years. They'll teach them how to handle a gun, how to deal with conflict. He could make a good officer."

Jack slammed two cups on the counter, his shoulder slumping. "You've lost your damned mind, you know that? That's what—four? Five years into the future? More if the kid goes for an associates degree in criminal justice. That doesn't help us *now*, Means." He turned, arms crossed in defiance, and glared at Tim. "*Now* we're relying on a vigilante to police our district. *Now* we don't have the money to hire a third officer and if we did, who? Clarence? He could do it,

153

but he's busy sewing everyone up. I can't keep doing this." He exhaled hard and just looked tired again. "Admit it, old man—neither can you."

This was what he got for waking Jack up early. But he didn't have a choice. Summer was going to bring Georgey home early this afternoon and there weren't any calls right now. He had to strike while the iron was hot.

He wasn't going to rise to the bait. Jack could be pissy, for all Tim cared. "Just because it's not an ideal solution doesn't mean we should ignore it entirely."

Jack's jaw tensed. Then the coffeemaker beeped and Jack turned around. He silently filled the cups, but at least he didn't slam the full mug in front of Tim and slosh hot coffee everywhere. "I know what this is about."

"Do you?" Damn.

"That certain older sister who's currently living in your house." Jack leaned forward. "She's pretty, isn't she?"

If Tim were the kind of guy to blush, he might have worked up the energy to heat his cheeks. But he'd been interrogating people for far too long to buckle at that weak line of attack. "She's taking care of her brother. It has nothing to do with me." Lies, all lies.

He should've figured Jack would guess the truth. Yes, he wanted Georgey to experience all facets of police work before he committed his life to law enforcement.

If Georgey went on a ride-along with Jack at night... Well, that left two consenting adults at home alone. Hell, he might even take off for the city and treat Summer to a fancy dinner before he brought her home and did a hell of a lot more than compliment her cooking.

He could take a night off and spend it in the arms of a beautiful woman who set his blood on fire. It would be like heaven.

Jack snorted. "Yeah, sure."

Even if Georgey worked out long-term, Jack was right—they couldn't keep doing this. "Do you have any better ideas? Qualified police officers don't exactly grow on trees around here."

Jack rubbed the back of his neck. "Do you know Ezra Johnson?"

Tim shook his head.

"He did two tours in Afghanistan, just landed back on the rez. Tammy and Clarence's older kid's dad. Kind of at loose ends. He has a high school diploma…"

Tim nodded. Although it'd been almost twelve years since Tim had gotten out of the service. He understood being at loose ends. "If he can do the job, I'll find some money to pay him." Somewhere. "But," he went on when Jack's eyes lit up, "make sure he can do the job. We don't need a severe case of PTSD wielding a gun around here."

"Done. And yeah, I'll take the kid on a ride-along. What night?"

Something loosened in Tim's chest in what felt like relief, but he made sure not to show it. Not Friday—that was too damned obvious. "Thursday?"

It was clear from the look Jack gave him that Tim wasn't fooling anyone. But he didn't care.

Summer Collins wasn't going to be here forever.

That was a fact—the pow wow was a few short months away. But she was here now. He'd be a damn fool if he didn't take her up on everything she had to offer and he didn't like to think he was a damned fool.

If it went well…maybe she'd come back. To visit, that was. Tim could live with seeing her smiling face every so often. It'd be enough.

"Fine," Jack said, taking a long sip of coffee. "But you still owe me."

"Done. Just make sure the kid doesn't get killed."

Jack grinned, and Tim saw a little of the coyote trickster in his eyes. "*That* means you'll owe me two."

***

Georgey was quiet on the way home. After a long day of confronting the failings of the public education system on the rez, Summer was more than happy to get lost in the world of the Percy Jackson audiobook.

She didn't know which was worse—the sheer number of kids who should've been in school who were instead struggling through a GED program barely equipped to handle their needs or the fact these were the kids who were willing to work. How many other kids had given up completely?

She wasn't ready for this. She wasn't ready for Georgey and his dyslexia and how she was supposed to feed and shelter him for at least another year, if not more. She wasn't prepared for the sheer lack of basic knowledge some of these kids had when they came in to study for their GED. She was lucky some of them knew how to read—and they didn't have dyslexia or any other obvious learning disabilities. They just…

They weren't stupid, although they talked of themselves as if they were, just like Georgey had. They simply hadn't been educated.

No, it was more than that. They didn't have any hope in them. Like one girl, who'd informed Summer her name was Circle, then glared as if daring Summer to laugh at it. Circle had looked Summer right in the eye when Summer explained she'd need to be able to write a persuasive essay and demanded to know, "What's the point?"

Summer had never felt less prepared for anything in her life than she had in that moment. She'd managed to fumble through some generic answer about taking care of yourself and getting a good job, but Circle just rolled her eyes and sat back, her arms crossed.

Summer wasn't sure she'd see the girl again.

That didn't even take into consideration Mrs. White Plume, the coordinator in charge of the GED program, who had been so happy to have another certified teacher to help tutor kids. As Mrs. White Plume had shaken Summer's hand, Summer felt like a life preserver someone had thrown to this kind, older woman, with a big smile and bigger hair. "It's just so important to have people come back," Mrs. White Plume had said, still pumping Summer's hand. "Show these kids there's life out there. With a little hard work, they can make it too."

But that felt like a lie. Summer wasn't coming back to the rez. She'd never been here to begin with. Instead, she'd been raised by a middle-class white woman in a mostly white town. She'd never needed a demonstration that there was potential to her life, something valuable in her education. It had been

157

expected—something that just *was*, like the air she breathed. She did well in school and the teachers encouraged her. She got assigned to tutor other kids and she enjoyed it. A career in education was a natural extension, an everyday thing for someone of her race and socioeconomic class.

Here? Here she was something rare and special and she wasn't sure she liked it. She shouldn't be noteworthy. She should be just another new teacher.

It was overwhelming, the responsibility of it all.

Finally they got to Tim's place. If this had been a regular day of teaching in Minneapolis, she'd pour herself an extra-big glass of wine and curl up with a book or Netflix. She might even splurge and order takeout. But here?

She had to figure out what they were eating for dinner, and she should talk to Georgey about the story they were listening to and make sure his comprehension was on target, and figure out a better answer to Circle's question and…

And she honestly didn't know if she was up to any of it.

Dragging, she followed Georgey into Tim's house and pulled up short when the scent of grilled meat hit her nose.

"Hey," Georgey said, "you never cooked like this for me."

"Yeah, well—I didn't like you then," Tim retorted. He looked past Georgey, and Summer almost staggered backwards—the heat in his eyes was that powerful.

"Does that mean you like me now?" Georgey asked, almost skipping over to the table.

"It means I need you well-fed if you're going to go on a ride-along with Jack on the night shift," Tim replied, not looking away from Summer.

A ride-along at night? Suddenly Summer wasn't exhausted. She practically vibrated with energy. Was he saying what she thought he was saying?

Georgey looked up from where he had a handful of fries shoved in his mouth. "When?"

"Don't talk with your mouth full," Summer said. *When* was an excellent question, however.

"Thursday," Tim said and a little smile played over his lips. It was just for her, that smile. It warmed her from the inside out.

Summer's heart leapt as Tim's gaze drifted to her lips and she knew he'd done this for her. They couldn't fool around with Georgey in the house—so Tim found a way to get the kid out.

"Thursday," she repeated and then smiled.

She wanted her summer fling.

She wanted him naked.

And in two days, she might just get to have him.

Chapter Twelve

The waiting was the hardest part. Summer concluded that as two of the longest days of her life trickled by in a slog of long drives to the other side of the reservation, tutoring reluctant students and working with Georgey on basic reading skills.

The good news was her brother was quite bright. That quickly became apparent as he got sucked into the world of Percy Jackson. He had no trouble following the story, no trouble answering her questions to test his comprehension. What's more, he was deeply excited about the story—which carried over when the novelizations came in the mail. The graphic novels were a lot of pictures and not very much text, but he was happy to sit down and try reading them, which was, as far as Summer could tell, a first.

She barely saw Tim for two days. He would drag in at seven or eight o'clock at night, looking beat. He'd inhale the dinner she'd made, ask Georgey how he was doing, then crash. It made the long days even longer.

She tried to be understanding about it. He was obviously putting in extra time to make sure Thursday was theirs. But it was frustrating.

She was frustrated. It had been a bit of a drought since her last boyfriend and she wasn't satisfied with lingering looks and stolen kisses. She wanted more from Tim. Much more.

Finally, Thursday evening rolled around. She hustled Georgey home a little earlier than normal and made sure he ate dinner before she said, "I'm going to take a shower."

She didn't rush. She shaved and exfoliated and washed her hair twice. She wanted to look great for Tim, which she found vaguely amusing because it wasn't like they hadn't been living together for a while. And she'd seen him when he was bruised and bloodied and almost too weak to stand.

But he'd healed. And she wanted to look pretty, dang it.

She was rinsing her hair when the bathroom door opened. "Georgey, give me a few more minutes," she snapped.

"The kid's gone," Tim's voice came from the other side of the shower curtain. "Jack picked him up five minutes ago."

Summer froze, then smiled. Who the heck cared about dinner? Tim was here and she was here and she was already naked. Was it too much to hope…

"Do you mind if I join you?" Tim said and Summer's heart took off at a gallop.

"Not at all."

She heard the sound of clothing hitting the ground as she rinsed her hair the last time. Then the shower curtain slid back and there was Tim.

For a moment, she just stared at him. She'd seen his chest, obviously, but there was so much more to

161

him. He was well built without being overly large, his dick half-hard against his leg. She moved aside to make room for him, but he didn't move at first. He only stared.

"Yes?" she asked, fighting the urge to self-consciously cross her arms in front of her breasts.

"You leave me breathless," he said, finally stepping into the shower.

Water ran over his shoulders, sluicing down the muscles of his chest. Summer exhaled, letting go of weeks of uncertainty and worry and stress so she could just be in this moment. Her breasts tightened as she slid her hands into his hair, tilting his head back so his hair was under the water.

"I thought this night would never come," she told him, turning him around so she could shampoo his hair. She'd never done this with anyone else and it was oddly intimate, that a man who wore a bulletproof vest and occasionally slept with a gun under his pillow would let her take care of him.

"I've been waiting for this since the moment you drove onto this rez," he said, his arms straight at his side, his hands curled into fists. She could see the tension in his shoulders as she massaged his scalp, but he held himself in check. "You weren't what I was expecting."

She laughed at that, recalling her mental image of an older man with white hair and a beer gut. "You weren't what I expected, either." She spun him around and ran the water over his hair. When that was done, she kept her hands on him, stroking the soap over his shoulders, down his chest. His dick stood at attention as she got closer, but she didn't want to rush this. They had all night, and frankly, she didn't care if she got dinner or not.

Breathless. She'd never left anyone breathless before. She'd dated—of course she had. She was twenty-six years old. But it seemed like most of the sex she'd had in college had been hookups. She was there, the guy was there, they were bored and horny and attracted to each other. It was simple and satisfying—to a point.

But it hadn't had a lot of romance. Since she'd started teaching high school, there hadn't been that easy availability. Now that time had passed, she realized she couldn't go back to casual hookups. She needed something more. Yes, she wanted that shaking, flying feeling of letting go and being completely satisfied.

But she needed something else, too. Leaving Tim breathless was a damn good place to start.

She soaped up his body, learning where the muscles cut in at his waist, that he was slightly ticklish on his stomach, that he had a jagged scar on his right knee that looked like it had been an extremely painful injury. And through it all, he stood there silently, fists clenched at his side, his breath coming faster and faster.

"Turn around," she demanded from where she crouched in front of him. He did so and she worked her way back up his body, taking the measure of his ass, kissing the scars on his back. Then she reached around and took hold of his erection, pressing her wet breasts against his back. He shuddered and leaned forward, bracing his hands on the shower wall as she explored his length and girth. When she cupped his stones, he groaned. "You're going to kill me, aren't you?"

She gave him a little squeeze and felt the shudder race through his body again. "Maybe. But it'll be slow." She dragged her thumb in a circle around his tip, causing him to gasp. "And you'll enjoy it."

Then he moved so quickly that she let out a squeak as he spun in her arms and backed her up against the wall. "You first," he growled. Growled!

Summer bit her lip to keep from smiling at him as her back made contact with the cool tile wall. "What did you have in mind?"

He leaned back just far enough that he could stare at her breasts, his eyes dark with hunger. "For starters, these." Then he bent his head and licked her right nipple.

Summer rested her head against the wall, losing herself in the sensation of his tongue swirling around her nipple. He sought out the other breast with his hand and began gently tugging on the tip until both were rock-hard. Steam filled the air as the water ran and ran, but she didn't care.

He was going to kill her and it would be slow and perfect and she would *absolutely* enjoy it.

He went from licking her breast to sucking on it, then he added teeth and began to nip at her. She couldn't help the little sounds that escaped her mouth. But she didn't care because they were alone in this house and if she wanted to moan and cry out as he worked her body, then she would.

The heavy weight between her legs grew heavier until she was close to the point of pain. "Please," she whimpered, lacing her fingers through his long, wet hair. "God, Tim—*please*."

He looked up at her, a wolfish grin on his face. "Please what?"

164

"You're driving me crazy," she told him, trying to pull him up so she could kiss him.

"Not the right answer," he said then he knelt in front of her. "Be specific. It makes things so much simpler, don't you think?"

"Are you lecturing me?" she asked in disbelief even as he pressed a kiss against her stomach. "Really, Tim."

He looked up at her and waited.

She shifted her hips, the tension inside her rising. "Fine. I need to come. There. Are you happy?"

"You always this bossy?" he asked as his hands dipped between her thighs and spread her legs apart.

"I *am* a high school English teacher," she reminded him but anything else she was going to say died on her lips as he pressed a kiss against her clit.

Summer shivered as waves of desire began to crest. His hair was wrapped around her fingers as she held him against her. With one hand, he spread her apart and nestled between her legs more fully. With the other, he stroked up and down over her opening.

"Oh, Tim—yes," she gasped as he began to lick her, his tongue moving in a slow, steady pace over her sex. She braced herself against the wall because otherwise, she might very well lose her balance and slide right to the floor of this shower.

"*Hm*," he hummed against her sensitive flesh, the vibrations driving her even more insane. One finger slipped inside, and she almost came right then. But he withdrew too quickly and she whimpered.

"Patience," he murmured, nipping at her thigh before turning his attention back to her swollen clit.

Patience? It'd been at least eight months since

165

she'd last gotten lucky. She was completely out of patience by now, and he was reducing her to nothing more than a tightly coiled spring of want and need.

But before she could find the words to tell him this, he slipped two fingers inside of her. Her muscles clamped down on him, and she felt like she was downing. He began to thrust his fingers in time with the movements of his tongue—a slow, maddening pace that was going to drive her over the edge. It was too much and not enough all at once. Her hips bucked against him as she pulled on his hair. "Tim," she demanded.

"Still not specific enough," he teased, then sucked her clit between his teeth, gently tugging on it until a cry pulled free from her chest.

Somehow, he held her up—because she sure as hell wasn't standing on her own anymore. Her legs had given out and all she could do was stare down at where his face was buried against her sex, his mouth surrounding her, his fingers driving into her. Then, without breaking the contact with her skin, he looked up at her through his dark lashes, and smiled against her skin, and without warning, the crisis broke and she came against him, wave after wave of desire washing over her.

Oh, it was a damn good thing he was holding her up. When her eyes focused again, he was still down there, still smiling against her skin, although he was now kissing her softly, his fingers slipping free of her.

Panting, she tried to smile but nothing seemed to be working quite right. "That was," she said, trying to untangle her hands from his wet hair, "*amazing*."

He smirked at her and said, "Babe, we're just getting started." Then he kissed his way back up her body, nipping at the soft skin underneath her belly button, lingering for long, glorious moments at her breasts. Finally, he brought his mouth back to hers. "You are the sweetest thing I've ever tasted," he told her, his voice shaking. Then his tongue swept inside her mouth.

She could taste herself on his lips, taste him underneath that. They tasted so damn *good* together.

His erection was hot and hard against her stomach, but he was in no hurry. And that too, was something different. In all those hookups in college, there'd been foreplay, sure. But…mostly it was her giving oral and very rarely receiving it. Guys her age didn't know how to seduce a woman properly. After all, there wasn't much seduction in Tumblr porn gifs.

But this? This was seduction, pure and simple. There was no hurrying before a roommate came back, no fumbling trying to find her clit. Tim was a man who knew what he was doing and how to do it well. He stroked his hands over her wet skin as he kissed her, tweaking her nipples and skimming between her legs, but he gave her time to come back down to earth.

It simply wasn't fair he was going to be good in bed—that he was already this good in the shower. It wasn't fair he cared about kids like Georgey, and this reservation, and the whole tribe, whether they wanted him to or not. It wasn't fair he was this gorgeous and intelligent and seemingly hell-bent on protecting her, on protecting them all.

God, she could love this man.

It simply wasn't fair she couldn't stay.

Chapter Thirteen

She really would be the death of him. Tim was trying to get to a place where he could last more than a minute or two, but she was demolishing any illusions of control he had. The whole time he kissed her, she touched him, too. She stroked his dick and pinched his flat nipples, palmed his ass and raked her nails down his back. She was trying to break him and he didn't know how much more he could take.

It turned out to be not much. When she cupped his stones again, he broke. With a growl, he spun her around. "Later," he said, nudging her legs apart with his knee, "I'm going to lay you out on the bed and make love to you properly."

Everything about her went tight and she moaned in what he hoped like hell was anticipation. The salty sweetness of her was still on his tongue and her ass flared out from her waist, begging for him to grab it. So he did. He dug his fingers into her flesh and spread her wide. She was the most beautiful woman he'd ever seen.

"What about now?"

The challenge in her voice was unmistakable. He was afraid he might have scared her with the intensity of his need—but he shouldn't have worried. And he did love a good challenge.

He bit her on the shoulder—not hard, but enough that she arched her back into him. "Now I'm going to fuck you."

She moaned, her head dropping against the wall. But then she straightened and said, "Condom?"

"Yeah." He reached out to where he'd set the condom on the edge of the sink. His hands shook as he rolled it on. It'd been so long—he didn't want to disappoint her. He'd wanted to go down on her—who the hell wouldn't? But he needed to remember how this went. Yeah, he was a little shaky.

He got the condom on and turned back to her. She hadn't moved, arms flat against the wall, her forehead resting on the tile, her legs spread wide. He covered her body with his and rubbed his dick against the crease of her sex. It didn't matter how long it'd been. There were some things that never changed and the way men and women fit together was one of them.

"So wet for me," he murmured in her ear as he fit himself against her. "Yeah?" Because he wanted to be sure.

"Yes," she whimpered, pushing back against him and taking the first inch inside of her.

As much as he wanted to watch his dick sink into her wet heat, he had to close his eyes because the feeling was so much *more* than he remembered. Her inner muscles gripped him tightly and it was all he could do to grit his teeth and hold on.

"You feel so good," she whispered, quietly enough he barely heard her over the water streaming against the back of his legs. "God, I've wanted this so much."

"Me too," he managed to get out. He flexed, then

169

he was buried in her. For a long moment, he just stood there, letting his body adjust, hanging onto his self-control by the thinnest of threads. She shifted against him, around him, and suddenly, he couldn't hold still any longer. He grabbed her by the hips and pulled out before thrusting back in as slowly and carefully as he could.

"*Oh*," she moaned, shifting so she was almost bent over at the waist, her hands still on the wall. It gave him a hell of a view. "Oh, yeah—like that."

She surrounded him, overwhelmed him. She was completely open to him, entirely vulnerable. If anyone ever tried to hurt her in any way, Tim would kill to keep her safe.

The ferocity of this realization knocked him off his rhythm for a moment.

But it was true. She was something rare and special, an outsider but also a member of the tribe, and a woman who looked at him and saw a man. Not the law, not an enemy—just a man. A man she liked. A man she trusted enough to be vulnerable with.

He would keep her by his side, if he could. Short of that, he would protect her with his life.

She moaned, thrusting her ass up against him harder and harder. His control snapped. He grabbed her ass, opening her wider, and watched as her body took him in again and again. He thrust hard and deep, gaining speed with every pump of his hips. He stroked one finger over the little rosebud of her ass, wanting to explore every part of her, but just then, she threw back her head and screamed out his name. "Tim—*Tim*!"

At the same time, her body tightened down on his and he couldn't hold on any longer. He came and came and *came* inside her until he went limp and collapsed against her back. He managed to pull out before he lost the condom, but that was as much moving as he could do. They stood there, water hitting him in the back of the legs, his forehead resting on her shoulders, panting. He wanted to laugh and tell her how perfect she was, and more than anything, he wanted to hold tight and never let her go.

He wasn't sure he could do any of that. So he just held her, his arms around her waist, her back against his chest. Minutes passed before she turned and threw her arms around his neck, burying her face against his chest. "God, Tim," she said in a shaky voice.

"Yeah." He didn't know what else to say because he was afraid if he talked, he might say something stupid, like asking her to stay.

But what could he offer her? A house, yeah—but it was small and the walls were thin and the door stuck and even if she was willing to overlook that, Georgey would be living on his couch.

Plus, he was still the law around these parts. He'd still have to gear up and take down gang bangers and arrest his own people and always be looking over his shoulder. The hours were hell, the job both brutal and boring. And she'd be stuck out in the middle of this rez, far away from her family and friends. The best she could hope for was a part-time gig at Sinte Gliske and that wasn't enough. Not for her.

It didn't matter how much he wanted her, how good they were together. She deserved someone who could give her 100% and that wasn't Tim. And there was no way he could follow her anywhere. He'd taken an oath.

Damn. He'd known this was short-term at best, but that was when he'd only liked and respected her and wanted her. Now that he'd had her—and would, God willing, have her again…

This was going to hurt. A lot.

Finally he got his brain unstuck. Tomorrow would come soon enough. Right now he had a beautiful woman in his arms and he'd made her feel good. Pride might be a sin but what the hell—they were naked in the shower.

Just then, the water heater gave out and the spray hitting his back turned ice cold. He yelped and she squealed, and somehow, they got out of the shower without slipping or falling.

She giggled and he couldn't help but smile as he wrapped a towel around her waist and kissed her firmly. "Come on," he said, keeping his voice light. If one night were all he got with her, he'd do his damnedest to make it a memorable one. "I promised you dinner."

***

Summer relaxed into the passenger seat, watching the last of the purple dusk fade into night.

"My apologies for the long drive," Tim said, his voice deep and rich. "But the only place to eat out on the rez is the gas station and you deserve something nicer than stale pizza."

She tried to fight the grin, but she lost the battle. Luckily Tim was focused on the road that stretched endlessly before them. "I've never had a dinner date at a drugstore before." Of course she had seen the signs for Wall Drug as soon as she'd hit the South Dakota state line. Free ice water and the world's largest jackalope were the highlights of the strangest tourist trap she had ever been in.

She and Tim had eaten buffalo burgers at a little diner and wandered through the various stores within the store, had their picture taken next to a miniature Mount Rushmore, and sat on the giant jackalope statue. It had been silly and fun and easy and, frankly, after the summer she'd had so far, that was exactly what she needed.

"Never let it be said that I don't know how to show a girl a good time." She could hear the smile in his voice.

"I can safely say I am having a *great* time." He'd unleashed amazing orgasms on her, then driven her to what was potentially the most amusing spot in the entire state, where he'd bought her dinner and ice cream. She hadn't had dates this fun in, well—she'd just leave it at *a long time*.

It had been a lovely surprise that the serious, intense sheriff of the White Sandy was capable of silliness, but he was. She had the picture of him fake-wrestling the jackalope to prove it.

She stared at him, his face little more than a silhouette in the darkness. Strong nose, strong jaw— everything about him spoke to his strength.

This was just a summer fling, nothing more. Fate had thrown them together and she wasn't too proud to take advantage of that happy accident. "How late will Georgey be out on his ride-along?"

It wasn't as if he moved, because she was pretty sure he hadn't. But somehow, anything relaxed or

173

easy-going about him had shifted right back to intensity.

More important, that intensity was focused on her.

"I don't know," he said, his voice low. Her nipples tightened in anticipation. "Why? Did you have something in mind?"

Honest to God, she went wet just listening to him. There was always a chance that the sex in the shower had been a one-off, a fluke. But she wasn't willing to risk that. She wasn't willing to only have him once. Nor would she be enthusiastic about waiting days or weeks until they could get Georgey out of the house again.

She had him all to herself *right now*. And she wasn't going to waste a single moment.

She unbuckled her seatbelt and leaned over the center console, running a hand up and down his thigh. "Something," she said, squeezing his leg close to his dick.

The car jerked a little to the left and immediately began to slow down. "Such as?" Tim gritted out as she palmed the hot length of his dick, already straining at his jeans.

The car dipped as he pulled onto the narrow shoulder, then he threw it into park. Summer sat up just long enough to look around, but they were in the middle of nowhere. There was no one on the road, no lights for as far as the eye could see. Just the night sky, the dark earth and the man next to her.

And it felt right. It felt good, being here with him. She wanted him again. More.

Luckily, she was going to have him. "You, me, significantly less clothing? Something like that?"

With a groan, he lifted her over the console. Her sundress bunched around her waist as she straddled him and she gasped as her clit came into contact with his erection.

"How about this?" he growled, pulling the sundress over her head and throwing it over his shoulder. With nimble fingers, he undid her bra and tossed that aside too.

"Something like this," she said breathlessly as he cupped her breasts and lifted them.

"Yeah, this will do," he said as his lips closed around her nipple. Her hips begin to shift of their own accord, grinding down on to him. She was wearing the cutest pair of panties she had packed, a lacy pink pair that were no match for his jeans and zipper.

"God, Summer," he said, switching to her other breast.

It felt dangerous to do this on the side of the road. Exciting, even. "One day," she gasped as he pinched her left nipple between his thumb and forefinger and pulled lightly, "I'm going to get you in a proper bed."

"I'd like that," he said, his other hand stroking down her back and over her bottom. His hand slipped underneath the edge of her panties and squeezed, rolling her hips forward, driving her against his hot erection harder, faster.

She sank her fingers into his hair and tilted his head up so she could kiss him. Even kissing him was something different, something new. The taste of coffee, with a hint of vanilla ice cream. Strong, with just a touch of sweetness. That was Tim Means.

But he was still too in control, still holding himself back. He was still in charge of things and she

175

wanted to strip that away and drive him just as mad as he drove her.

So she ground down on him at the same time she bit his neck, right where it met his shoulder. She tugged with her teeth—hard, but not hard enough to leave a bruise.

Probably.

It worked. "Out of the car," he growled, throwing open his door. "*Now*."

Yeah, it might take a lot to make him lose control—but right now? He didn't have a single bit of it. She grinned as he stood, carrying her with him. Her legs went around his waist and the humid night air brushed over her bare skin.

She didn't care that they were on the side of the road, where anyone could see them. All she could feel was this aching need to have him inside her. She needed him, needed the freedom that only he could give her.

It wasn't wrong to want this. She had to believe that.

"Do you see what you do to me?" Tim asked, his voice low and raw. It set every one of her nerve endings on fire.

Darkness touched him with deep shadows, but there was no missing the hunger in his eyes. The intensity she saw there made her body shiver with anticipation. She was in too deep and there was no going back now.

"There was a music video when I was growing up," he said, backing her up until his body had hers pinned against the hood of his car.

She arched her back, thrusting her breasts up

toward him. "Do you want me to dance for you?" She was breathing hard and she knew if he asked, she would. Nude, in the middle of the road, she'd climb up on the hood of his cop car and give him a hell of a show.

She was a long way from the mild-mannered high school English teacher Ms. Collins right now and she'd never felt better.

"No time." He did away with her panties and pulled back only long enough to grab a condom out of his pocket. "Later, I'll make sure there's foreplay and kissing. But not now. I need you too much right now, babe."

She moaned and writhed underneath him, clutching at his shoulders and arms for balance as she slid over the smooth surface of the car hood.

Then he was against her, inside her, thrusting into her wet heat. Summer cried out his name and he managed to pause, staring down at her. "Jesus, you're so beautiful," he moaned before leaning down to capture her lips in a kiss. He thrust forward again and the orgasm ripped through her. All she could think was *there he is*—the man she wanted to spend the rest of her life with.

Then a new emotion shot through her—one she didn't want but didn't know what to do with because he was still buried inside her.

Fear.

Because she might damn well love this man—but how could it work? How could any of this work?

"Stay with me," he murmured against her chest before he flicked his tongue over her nipple.

She gasped. Was he saying—

177

"Just stay in the moment, love," he went on and she didn't know whether to cry or laugh. "Don't overthink it. This ain't no thinking thing."

At that, she did laugh, a sated, happy sound. Sex with him was a joy, one she didn't know if she'd ever get enough of. She stroked his cheek, her body still shimmering with the aftershocks of the orgasm. "I'm right here with you," she told him, threading her fingers through his hair. "Nowhere else I'd rather be." Then she lifted her hips up, pulling him deeper.

He took hold of her hand and held her palm to his cheek before kissing the inside of her wrist. Through it all, he stared down at her as if he were trying to memorize every detail—just in case.

The sadness in his eyes stole her breath away. "Tim?" Summer tried to push herself up on her elbows. "What is it?"

But he just shook his head and hauled her against his chest, holding her tight. She locked her legs around his waist and for a perfect moment, they were together. She wasn't lonely and he wasn't, either. It made her eyes water with joy, with sadness. What only made it worse was she could feel waves of emotion rolling off him, too.

God, she'd miss him when she left. But there she went again, thinking. He was buried inside her and she was nude on the hood of his car and now was the time to feel, dammit. But she couldn't ignore their connection.

So she skimmed her teeth over his neck. "It's all right," she whispered in his ear, her heart bursting with a whirlwind of emotion. "Because I feel it too."

"Right here, right now, you're perfect," he said as

he laid her down on the car hood again. This time, he didn't hold back. He pounded into her body and nipped at her lips, her neck, tugged on her nipples until her cries of pleasure filled the night as he pushed her body over the edge again and this time, he followed her.

They lay locked together, panting hard, for a long time. Oh, holy hell, she just didn't have any words, dammit. All she had were feelings and she didn't have a clue how to describe them out loud. So she said nothing while he held her and gloried in her holding him.

Finally, when she was sure she could say words that weren't *I love you* or *I want to stay with you*, she spoke. "That was a pretty good fantasy. Whitesnake, right?"

He pushed himself off her chest, grinning wildly. She did that. She made him look so happy. "Right."

Finally—almost reluctantly—he pulled free of her. She sagged against the car hood, her mind feeling like it was coated in a thick layer of mud.

He lay on top of her, both of them breathing hard. Summer held him against her breast, staring up at the night sky and its dazzling stars.

Even when she had imagined the summer fling, it hadn't been this good. This *perfect*. Because it hadn't been Tim Means.

He leaned back enough to stare down at her, his lips quirked into a smile that looked shocked. "I can't believe we just did that."

She arched against him, stretching her arms over her head and putting her breasts at their best advantage. "It was rather amazing, wasn't it?"

"You're amazing," he said, cupping her breasts and brushing his thumbs over her nipples. "I want you in my bed tonight. I want to wake up with you in the morning."

She gasped at the sweet words, made all the sweeter by how damn serious he sounded.

"Even though you're not exactly a ray of sunshine first thing in the morning," he added with a smirk.

She swatted at his arms and they both laughed. But then she remembered what sleeping in his bed would mean. She could wake up with his arms wrapped around her—but in the very next room, Georgey would be on the couch. "But…"

"I don't care," Tim said, pushing back and helping her sit up. She needed the help, too. After that orgasm, her muscles felt like jelly. "He already knows there's something going on between us. He's protective of you, but then, so am I. I just want to hold you, Summer. We don't have to have crazy sex when he's around. We can always come out here." He looked up, where the night sky twinkled in what seemed like amusement. He took a deep breath and looked at her. Even in the darkness, she could see the want in his eyes. She could feel her body answering with the same desire.

It only got worse when he stepped back between her legs and cupped her face in his palms. "I know we don't have much time, babe. I don't want to waste a minute of it simply because of what the snot-nosed teenager might say. I want you for as long as possible."

Summer wasn't sure if she had ever been in love before. Lust, yes. She had cared deeply for a few of her boyfriends. But this?

This was so much more. Tim wasn't a boy playacting at being a man. He didn't duck responsibility—either in his job or in bed.

Or on the car.

He cared deeply about his people, about Georgey and, it seemed, about her.

All of that would've been enough to make her fall for him. Because she was falling for him. But that wasn't solely who he was. He was still a man who could take a girl for ice cream and take silly pictures with giant statues of imaginary creatures.

She touched her forehead to his and covered his palms with hers, holding him close. "When I'm with you, I'm not lonely anymore." That was the truth.

She was perfectly fine being by herself. But she knew what it was to feel alone even when she was out with a group of friends. Especially when she was visiting her mother.

"You feel it, too?" he murmured, sounding awe-struck and nervous and hopeful, all at once. "Something more?"

Something more. That's what Tim was. "I do."

"Stay with me tonight."

She sighed as she kissed him. She shouldn't want more than a night or even a summer at a time. All she could ask for was what he was offering.

So she took that—and nothing more. "I will."

"Good.

***

After that, they settled into something that felt like a routine.

181

Sarah M. Anderson

Three days a week, Summer took Georgey with her when she drove out to Sinte Gliske community college. She didn't exactly have a lesson plan for him—he needed help in everything, so she tutored him in whatever she was tutoring another student. It wasn't the most educationally sound way to approach things, but he was making progress. At the very least, he was trying and that was more than she'd been afraid he might be able to do. They listened to audiobooks in the car and went over the graphic novels during dinner and talked about life in Minneapolis.

Tim was right. She couldn't stay. And if Georgey wanted to have a shot in hell at an education and a life, he couldn't stay either.

Two days a week, Tim took Georgey on a ride-along. The kid seemed honestly excited about the idea of being a cop. And there was no denying the bond between him and Tim. Georgey was basically an unpaid deputy intern at this point and frankly, having a goal and a mentor was good for him.

How long had it been since there'd been a man Georgey could look up to? Their father had died so long ago… Had her brother had anyone since then?

Those afternoons, Tim would drop Georgey off at the childcare center to help after nap time until Summer got back from either the community college or a grocery run. She bought a lot of groceries. She could see Georgey growing and filling out before her eyes, putting on muscle and growing into his hands and feet.

But for his sudden size, he was still a kid at heart. When she came to get him at the center, he was usually out running around the makeshift soccer field, coaching his team with lots of cheers and high fives.

Sometimes she would sit in the car and watch. Little kids would tackle him when something exciting happened, nearly knocking him over with their exuberance. There was something so familiar about that. She remembered Georgey as a toddler, running into her at top speed because he was happy to see her and how she would pick him up and spin him around, trying not to drop him while he squealed with delight.

She wished they didn't have to go. She wished she didn't have to take him away from the only family he'd known. She wished her mother hadn't kept her away from this, either.

But that was in the past. In the future, there wasn't any other way forward.

Through it all, she enjoyed her time with Tim Means. Because he made time for her.

One night a week, Jack, the other deputy, would take Georgey for a nighttime ride-along. Tim was training someone named Ezra to be a third deputy and on those nights, Ezra was the backup. For one night of the week, Summer had Tim all to herself.

Sometimes they drove to Wall or Rapid City to see a movie and eat out. Or they did silly things like play miniature golf or go to a bar to throw darts or play pool. They even caught a concert one weekend, all the way up in Sturgis, surrounded by bikers. And it was fun. Crazy, exciting—all those things she'd wanted out her summer fling, she got with Tim, and more.

And then, on the way home? Tim would find some deserted back road and make every single one of her fantasies come to life. She rode him in the back seat, pinning his hands over his head and nipping at the skin along his shoulders until he groaned with the best kind of pain. He bent her over the hood of his car, landing a playful swat or two on her ass as he buried himself inside her. Once, she had his zipper down and his shorts shoved aside before he even got the car in park. She'd blocked his attempts to pull her mouth off him until he had spurted his release down her throat.

Then, as punishment, he'd all but thrown her onto the roof of his car so she was right at his eye level. When she'd shattered under his tongue and his fingers, he hadn't let up. Instead, he nipped and sucked and licked harder, faster, making her cry out and then scream as she broke again and then a third time.

The house, they shared with Georgey.

But the night sky was theirs and theirs alone.

She *had* to leave. But how was she going to? How could she walk away from a man like Tim Means?

She didn't know. But she needed to figure it out, and quickly.

The pow wow—the unofficial end of summer and her time on the White Sandy—was less than a week away.

Chapter Fourteen

Hey, there's Circle!" With that, Georgey was off like a shot, cutting through the crowd.

"Georgey? Come back when you're hungry!" Summer yelled after him.

Tim chuckled. "That'll only be ten minutes, babe." He wasn't holding her hand and that drove him nuts. But it was her choice. After an initial awkward week or so, where she'd tensed any time Georgey acknowledged she and Tim were sharing a bed, she'd relaxed a bit. At the very least, she'd stopped flinching every time Georgey smirked at her, which counted for a lot.

But somehow, Tim knew she wouldn't be comfortable advertising their relationship to the tribe at large. So he hadn't touched her since he'd handed her out of the car fifteen minutes ago.

That didn't mean she wasn't the focus of his attention. Summer Collins walked around the pow wow with a look of joy on her face that was both familiar yet entirely new. "It's so much *more* than I remember," she said softly.

"Yeah?" To him, the pow wow was the same as it'd ever been.

The dance circle was open underneath the wide blue sky. Along one half of the circle, a semi-permanent

Sarah M. Anderson

shelter had been jerry-rigged and the drummers sat in the coolest part. The group of men—mostly older grandfathers—were still squabbling over who was drumming when. Children in their fancy dance outfits darted among the crowd and under a stand of pines, a group of grandmothers were cooking up fry bread. Women and men in their outfits smiled and preened, adjusting their horsehair roaches or feathers.

Tim stood in the middle of it all, breathing in deeply. This was his place, his people. He belonged here, among the chaos and laughter and noise. It was familiar and comforting. No matter what shit went down during the week, the pow wow was when they all came together.

He looked down at Summer. Eyes wide, she took everything in. He only wished she belonged here, too.

"I guess I just remember playing with Georgey," she explained. "And listening to the drums while my dad told stories," she said in that quiet voice as a grass dancer pushed past her to line up for the opening dance. "I don't really remember all the dancers."

"Hey Sheriff, Summer," Jenna, the nursing student at the Clinic, said as she hurried to her place in line, her dress covered in tinkle cones that jingled softly with every move. "Having fun?"

Summer's mouth about fell open. "Jenna! Your dress is *amazing*."

"Thanks!" Jenna called over her shoulder, jingling louder as she hurried.

"Jenna competes in the women's fancy dance category at the state level," Tim told Summer. "When she's not working at the Clinic, that is. She won scholarships that helped pay for her nursing education."

186

Summer looked up at him. "Do you dance?"

He snorted. "Only the opening dance these days—it's intertribal. Anyone can dance."

Her mouth rounded into a nearly perfect *O* as she inhaled sharply. "Anyone?"

Tim didn't like to think he was a stupid man, and only the stupidest would miss the obvious excitement in her eyes. He bowed at the waist. "May I have the honor of escorting you in this dance, Summer Collins?"

"I'd love to, Tim Means," she said, a pretty blush darkening her cheeks.

"Then let's get you outfitted."

He led her over to where the Tall Trees and Thunder families had laid out their blankets. Anyone would have loaned him the necessary stuff, but he knew Summer would be most comfortable with Tammy Thunder. The two women had become friends while Georgey played with the kids at the Child Care Center.

Next to the Thunders, Melonie Bodine had a blanket laid out. She was helping Jamie, the boy she'd adopted with Nobody, with his feathered bustle. Tim wasn't sure if the kid had danced before, but if Melonie and Jamie were here, that meant Nobody couldn't be far away.

Funny how that thought didn't bother Tim as much as it might have.

True enough, the Tall Trees women welcomed Summer with open arms. Flo Tall Trees insisted Summer take her shawl, a deep blue with rainbow fringe along the edge. Tara, the receptionist at the Clinic, helped Summer drape the shawl over her

187

shoulders so the fringe lined up perfectly along the bottom before her daughter Nelly needed help with her jingle dress.

"Hey," Tim said, standing out of the way next to Clarence Thunder, who was putting the finishing touches on his son Mikey's bustle. "Congratulations on your daughter."

The big man stood and beamed at his wife and baby. "Thanks, man. Tammy was just happy she could make it out today—you know how much she loves to watch Mikey dance."

Tim nodded as Tammy, with her newborn daughter Farrah on her shoulder, showed Summer how to step carefully to make the fringe all swing the same way at the same time.

"She's really fitting in," Clarence said quietly to Tim as the women found an extra beaded comb to stick in Summer's hair. "Tammy loves her."

So did Tim.

The realization rocked him back. He had fallen head over heels for Summer Collins. Which was something rare and wonderful yet also tinged with sadness. "She's leaving soon. And taking Georgey with her."

Clarence thought about that for a minute. "She's going to get the kid through school?"

"Yeah." Wasn't that the problem? What was best for Tim wasn't the same thing that was good for Georgey.

"Think the kid will come back?"

"Might." He might not. Summer and Georgey might very well drive off this rez, never to be heard from again. Or at least not for a decade or so.

Just like the last time Summer left.

Not that it was Summer's fault. That was her mother's doing, Tim was pretty sure. "I think Georgey's planning on joining the army, doing a few tours, maybe looking at law enforcement."

Tim had never had a kid. He'd been on his own since, well, since he'd been Georgey's age. But he had to admit, he felt a certain amount of pride that the kid was considering following in his footsteps.

But would Georgey join the force here? Or somewhere else? Would he be an Urban Indian or would he come back to the grass and the sky?

Didn't matter. Wherever that kid went, they'd still be family. Always.

Clarence stepped forward to take his daughter from his wife. The baby was so small against the giant man's shoulder, Tim couldn't help but grin at the pair of them.

"We left," he reminded Tim, patting his tiny baby with a gentle hand. Tim ducked around to see the little one was fast asleep. "We left and we came back. So did she," he added, nodding his head at the women.

Tim turned to see Summer, her hair braided with the comb in it, the shawl draped over her shoulder. Damn, she took his breath away. Right now, he couldn't see the woman he'd met months ago, lost and a little afraid of what she might find on the rez.

Instead? Summer fit here. She fit in with the tribe. She belonged next to him. Behind her, Tammy, Tara and Flo all beamed widely. Tara, in particular, was giving him A Look.

"Well?" Summer asked, spinning once for him, the fringe rippling out from her shawl.

189

Damn it all, he was completely in love with her. And he wasn't fooling anyone.

How was he going to let her go?

The announcer called for the dancers for the opening dance, so Tim forced those depressing thoughts away. "You look perfect," he told her, guiding her toward the end of the line.

They lined up behind the competitors and waited while Rebel Runs Fast and the Catholic preacher from the far side of the rez gave the opening prayers. Then the drumming started and the crowd shuffled into the circle.

"The grass dancers go first," Tim said, leaning down to explain the dance to her. "They flatten the grass down for the rest of us. They also dance like they're hunting through the tall grass. Then the fancy dancers, the jingle dancers and the women's traditional, then the shawl dancers, then the kids."

He was surprised to see Jacob Plenty Holes, with his eye patch, lining up with his daughter Kip Two Elks, the little girl in a huge hat and sunglasses to protect her albino eyes from the noon sun. Jacob rarely joined these things. Tim nodded when he caught Jacob's eye and Jacob nodded back.

Summer craned her neck around. "Then us?"

"Then us—tribe members who aren't competing—and anyone from another tribe or other outsiders."

The drummers hit the skin drum and their voices rose in the lilting song and finally, Tim and Summer danced into the circle.

It always amazed Tim how the rhythm could come back to him after months or years away. He'd only been home on the rez for a few weeks after he gotten out of the Army when there'd been a pow wow and he almost hadn't danced because he wasn't sure he still could. The Army had turned him into a solider but it had stripped away some of what made him a Lakota.

But the moment he'd heard that drum beat, he'd let go a breath he hadn't realized he'd been holding in for years and his feet found the grass and he'd known then—he'd come home.

That same feeling of belonging hit him again as he moved alongside Summer. He watched her out of the corner of his eye as they moved slowly around the circle, the song reaching its crescendo. She took it all in, grinning and waving when one of the little kids from the center recognized her.

He didn't want her to leave, but he hoped like hell she'd know she could always come home.

Back to him.

When the song ended, the circle cleared. "I'll take these things back to Tammy and Tara," she told him. "But I didn't see Georgey in the circle."

Tim mentally translated that statement. "I'll check on him," he said and forgot she didn't like public displays of affection because he leaned down and brushed a kiss over her lips. Her cheeks darkened but she didn't pull away. "Wait for me with the Tall Trees, okay? Then we'll get some fry-bread tacos. Heaven on a plate."

She nodded and, blushing furiously, managed a graceful turn that sent her fringe swaying along with her hips. Tim watched her walk away and then, when the crowd swallowed her up, turned and caught Rebel watching. The medicine man had the nerve to wink.

Tim rolled his eyes and settled back into his usual

191

role—watching from the edges of the tribe, keeping his eye out for anything out of the ordinary. Pow wows were big family affairs, something everyone looked forward to—but sometimes drama spilled over into violence, especially later in the evening, when people started drinking after they'd competed.

But right now, the sun was high in the sky and the biggest risk was someone eating too much fry bread and getting sick. Tim made a circuit around the outside of the dance circle, keeping an eye out for Georgey.

He spotted the boy with Circle, standing back by a pickup truck crowded with other teens. Tim kept his distance. Georgey wouldn't want it to look like Tim was his babysitter in front of his friends—and besides, some of those kids? They were known to run with the Killerz. Georgey might be able to pick up some valuable gossip—as long as Tim didn't barge in and chase everyone off.

So he kept moving until he got back to where the Tall Trees and Thunder families had set up camp. Flo was in her lawn chair and Tammy was nursing her daughter under the shade of a beach umbrella. Tim made sure to avert his eyes.

But that was it. Clarence was probably at the drum circle and Tara with the older kids. And Summer?

"Where's Summer?"

Tara looked up, her brow furrowed with concern. "I haven't seen her since you led her into the circle."

Flo added, "I thought she was with you?"

"I went to check on Georgey—she said she was coming back here to return the shawl." A prickle of unease made the hairs on the back of his neck stand up.

Not that he was worried. Summer was a grown woman. She didn't have to let him know where she was at all times. Besides, she'd probably run into Dr. Mitchell or something. Rebel was here, after all, which meant his wife was probably scowling at people even as she smiled.

"Well, tell her I'm looking for her," he said, turning away.

"She's a sweetheart," Flo called after him.

Tim wanted to agree—but he wanted to find Summer more. That prickle of unease was getting pricklier by the damned minute.

He made another circuit around the dance circle, where the grass dancers were timing their steps to the irregular beat of the drums. He was three-fourths of the way around when he ran into Rebel again. "Please tell me Summer is with your wife," he said without any other introduction.

Rebel gave him a worried look. "Madeline isn't here. Problem?"

"Just a feeling." He didn't explain because, if there were one man on this rez who would understand a bad feeling, it was Rebel.

"You go this way, I'll go that way." Rebel took off without another word.

Tim didn't have time to be grateful. With every second that ticked by, he got closer to straight-up dread.

Where the hell had she gone? It wasn't like she'd been here long enough to make enemies. From what Georgey said, the kids she tutored at Sinte Gliske thought Summer was really nice and heaven knew the kids and parents from the Child Care Center thought she and Georgey were a godsend. Everyone liked her.

But not everyone liked him.

And, despite her discomfort with public displays of affection, it was common knowledge she and Georgey were staying with him. That she was *with* him.

When he spotted a grass dancer in full regalia hurrying away from the dance circle next to a woman with light brown hair and a blue shawl around her shoulders, every single one of his senses kicked into high gear.

There she was. Thank God.

But the relief at finding her was short-lived. Who the hell was she with? All the grass dancers were in the circle. Something was wrong, he realized, dread dumping adrenaline into his system. This was not good. Not good at all.

It only got worse when Georgey stepped out in front of the grass dancer. The bottom dropped out of Tim's stomach.

Sunlight glinted off a gun. Pointed at Georgey.

Tim bellowed in rage and took off at a dead run.

***

"No," Summer whispered in horror as the man in the dance costume leveled a second gun at her baby brother. A minute ago, she might've said having a stranger jam a gun against her side and tell her to move was the scariest thing that had ever happened to her.

But now she knew—being forced to stand next to the stranger while he apparently debated shooting Georgey was by far the most terrifying thing she'd ever seen.

194

"Shit, Levi—what the hell are you doing?" Georgey said. His eyes were wide but that was the only sign he was even a little concerned at this development.

Summer was beyond concerned. She was about to have a panic attack. *Keep an eye on your brother.* That was literally the only thing her father had asked of her.

But how was she supposed to do that? This guy was armed to the teeth! She wasn't a black belt. She'd never defended herself from anyone more dangerous than drunk, handsy guys at a bar.

"Dude," Georgey said again, still sounding damnably calm, as if this were part of the afternoon's festivities. The steady rhythm of the drumming filled the air. She tried to get her heart to beat at the same pace, but that was a lost cause. "This is not the smartest thing you've ever done."

In and amongst the panic, Summer was proud for her brother standing up to this guy. Terrified he was about to get shot, but proud nonetheless.

"It's the middle of the day and everyone's here," Georgey went on, waving a hand around the pow wow. Off to the side, the kids he must have been hanging out with were watching the proceedings with a cautious interest. Why weren't they going for help? Why were they just watching? "Kidnapping her? Did you honestly think you were going to walk right out of here?"

"Shut the fuck up, Georgey," Levi hissed. "You sold me out, man. Sold out the Killerz. Went running to that asshole Tim and that fucking *sica* Nobody. Nobody doesn't come out in daylight and I can handle that old man."

Summer made eye contact with Circle. *Get help*, she tried to say with her eyes. Circle had come back to tutoring several times and she obviously liked Georgey. If anyone in this group would get help, it'd be her.

The girl nodded, bless her heart, and slipped backwards.

"I sold you out?" Georgey's voice cracked with indignation. "What the hell are you talking about? You shot Shorty!"

Summer wasn't sure because she couldn't hear much over the rush of blood pounding in her ears, but she *felt* a hush fall over the kids watching this exchange.

Georgey must have felt it, too, because he seemed to physically grow right before her eyes. Bigger. Meaner. And pissed as hell. "You shot Shorty in the ass, man. He's just a kid. A little kid who looked up to you and what did you do to deserve his respect? You told him to run and then put a bullet in him like he was nothing. Nothing but target practice."

Levi made a high-pitched noise that was almost a laugh. The sound sent another chill down her back because that was not a noise a sane, well-adjusted person made.

Shit, this Levi was going to kill them all.

"You sold *us* out, man," Georgey went on, his voice vibrating with rage. "You put your own people in danger and for what? Guns? Drugs? You're no warrior," Georgey said, his voice getting meaner—and louder. "Put the gun down, Levi."

Levi was clearly in no mood for this because he jabbed the one in Summer's ribs even harder. Summer winced and aimed an imploring look at Georgey. Quit pissing the armed madman off!

"You stupid whelp," Levi seethed. "Get the fuck out of my way or I shoot her *and* I shoot you. You could've been a Killerz, man. We could've been your family."

Georgey's eyes flashed. "We are all family," he intoned in a damned respectable imitation of Tim's favorite refrain. "Even when we do stupid shit like attempted kidnapping and gun running. But if you hurt my sister, I will *end* you."

"Georgey, no," Summer pleaded. She couldn't just stand here and watch this asshole shoot her brother. "Just get out of his way."

"Levi? Did you kill Shorty? Is that why he hasn't been around?"

Summer didn't know who spoke—she couldn't look away from Georgey. But the question at least accomplished one goal—Levi swung sideways. He kept the one gun against her side and the other pointed in Georgey's general direction, but at least he had a better chance of missing at this angle.

"I didn't kill that crybaby," he snarled, sounding less stable by the second. "You can't kill a kid with rat shot. I just needed to teach him a lesson. Because that's what happen when you betray the Killerz." He swung back to Georgey, the gun leveled at her brother's chest. "But I shot the wrong kid, didn't I?"

Time slowed down. At least, that was how it felt to Summer. Levi took aim at the same second that a little kid—no more than five and dressed in a miniature dance outfit like Levi's—ran between Levi and Georgey. The drum beat pulsed through the air and the hair on the back of Summer's neck rose as electricity raced through the air. Someone screamed— Summer and maybe someone else.

Georgey yelled, "Jeremy! No!" at the same instant he dove for the kid, at the same instant Levi pulled the trigger. The gun roared.

Lots of screaming. Red bloomed on Georgey's shoulder.

Someone grabbed Summer's arm, the one away from Levi's gun, and spun her away from Levi. Levi was jerked backward at the same instant a huge shape rushed at him from the side, knocking the arm with the gun that'd shot Georgey up into the air. Lightning struck. Another gunshot tore through the afternoon air.

Then Summer was sprawled in the dirt, a body on top of her and a man yelling, "Stay down!" in her ear.

"Georgey!" she sobbed. Her baby brother had been shot!

She'd failed. Her dad had asked her to keep the kid safe and she'd failed him. All of them.

"Rebel? Call your wife, man."

The man on top of her moved. "How bad?"

"Through and through. But we'll need to get him patched up."

"Him? Him who?" she demanded as Rebel rolled off her. Because there were a lot of *hims* present.

She sat up to survey the scene. Clarence, the big nurse from the Clinic, knelt next to Georgey. Tim and Nobody Bodine had Levi face-first in the dirt. Tim was tying Levi's arms behind his back and Nobody had a foot on Levi's neck. Circle had Jeremy, the little dancer, in her arms. A strange sort of electricity pulsed through the air.

The drumming stopped and a silence that felt absolute fell over them all.

No, she wanted to cry. But she couldn't because that was the exact moment she realized that everyone she loved was right here and she might have just watched her brother die.

"Jeremy's okay, right?"

Summer choked out a sob at the sound of Georgey's voice. He was alive. Hell, he didn't even sound that upset.

"Yeah," Circle said. "Scared, but okay. Can I take him to find his mom, Sheriff Means?"

"Wait for Rebel," Tim said, finishing his knot. "I have to deal with *this*," he added, scorn dripping off his words as he leaned his knee onto Levi's back, "but I'll call her to explain. Might be a few hours."

Summer inhaled sharply. She'd never seen Tim this furious. But instead of a wild, uncontrolled rage, Tim was ice cold.

Or he was, until he looked at her. His eyes gave him away. "You okay?" he asked, somehow managing to sound worried and tender and perfect even as he leaned against Levi harder, making the asshole whine with pain.

She nodded because she wasn't sure she remembered how to speak. Somehow, she got to Georgey's side. Clarence had rolled him over and a ring of blood was spreading across his chest like waves rippling in a pond. The big man was holding what looked like a balled-up t-shirt to Georgey's shoulder.

Georgey's face was creased with pain but he asked, "Who else was hit?" in the same voice he might

199

have asked what was for dinner. "There were two shots, right? Did he get anyone else?"

"Why is everyone so calm?" Summer demanded. Georgey had been shot, for God's sake! How could he even think of someone else at a time like this?

"Shit, Levi—you hit my tire! Where the hell am I going to get a new tire?" asked a pissed-off teenager.

"Better the tire than your leg," Clarence noted helpfully. "Rebel?"

"She's on her way to the Clinic." If anything, Rebel sounded bored by this whole situation. "If you don't need me, I'll go with Circle to take Jeremy back."

The little boy, his headdress barely hanging on his head, pushed up next to Summer to stare at Georgey. "You okay?"

"He's fine," Clarence said. "He'll have a super-awesome scar, though."

"Cool," Jeremy said in awe even as tears clung to the ends of his eyelashes.

Circle knelt by Georgey's head. "That was amazingly bad-ass," she whispered before brushing a kiss over his lips.

"Why is everyone so calm?" Summer demanded again, the hysteria rising. Even the little kid was acting like this was no big deal! "He's bleeding!"

"That's our cue," Clarence said and damn him, he said it calmly. "Summer, you come to this side and hold here." With his chin, he pointed at the t-shirt. "I'll pick him up and we'll meet the doc at the clinic. He's going to be fine."

"Bad-ass scar," Georgey said weakly.

Clarence lifted and Georgey went pale. Somehow

Summer managed to keep the pressure on his shoulder without blacking out. "You're okay," she repeated over and over. She had no idea if she was trying to convince him or herself.

"I'll call Jack," she heard Tim say. "Can you get him to the jail without killing him?"

She didn't know who he was talking to, but there was another little pop of electricity that she didn't understand at all.

Levi screamed and said, "Don't you dare leave me with this fucking *sica*! This is police brutality, man!"

"You shot a kid," Tim said, disgust dripping off every word. "Nobody doesn't like it when someone hurts a kid, does he?"

"Keep moving," Clarence said and Summer had no choice but to follow him, tripping sideways over her feet as she struggled to keep up with Clarence's huge strides.

"Georgey? You're going to be fine," she repeated. "You idiot. Why did you piss him off like that?"

"Was...waiting. For Tim. Made a promise," he muttered, his skin ashen. Now that he wasn't in front of Circle and his friends, he wasn't bothering to put on a brave face. "Kept it."

"What promise, sweetie?"

"Told Dad I'd keep an eye..." His head lolled against Clarence's huge shoulder. "On you," he finished and then his body went limp.

"Georgey?"

"He's fine," Clarence assured her. "Just passed out. Moving isn't fun for him right now. Here's my truck. You'll have to ride with him in the back."

Before Summer could protest, strong hands went around her waist and boosted her into the truck bed. "I'm here, babe. I'm right here."

Tim. She cried with the relief of it all.

Things happened in a blur. Someone threw a blanket into the back of Clarence's truck and she spread it out. Together, Clarence and Tim laid the unconscious Georgey out. Summer cradled her brother's head in her lap while Tim put pressure on the wound, both front and back. They drove way too slowly for Summer's taste, like there wasn't a wounded teenager in the back of the truck, turning horrifying shades of gray even as the rags Tim held against his wounds turned bright red and then darker brown.

"You kept your promise," Summer wept as she braced Georgey's head from another bump. "I'm sorry I didn't keep mine."

"He's not going to die," Tim said. "Babe? Look at me." Summer had no choice but to do as he ordered. "He's going to be fine."

She nodded. Clarence had said the same thing, hadn't he? They wouldn't lie about something life or death, would they?

"But," Tim went on, sorrow in his eyes, "you're leaving as soon as you can. And you'll take Georgey with you. Just to be safe."

He didn't say *because there might be gang retribution*, but he didn't have to. Summer understood. Levi was in deep with gangs. He might have even been the one who shot Tim in the bullet-proof vest at the gang fight all those weeks ago. Things might get messier and more dangerous before the day was out.

There would be no staying just one more day, no dragging things out. She would take Georgey to Minneapolis, to the safety of anonymity that came with living in the big city. Because that was the only way she could keep her promise to their father. Just like Georgey had kept his.

Which meant she would leave Tim. If not today, then tomorrow.

This was how things ended.

With a bang under the wide blue sky.

"I'm sorry, babe," he whispered. "I wish you could stay."

"I wish I could, too," she wept. "I'm in love with you and right up until the guns and the blood, I'd felt like I'd finally found a place I could call home." She made herself look at him, at the man who'd risked everything to keep her brother out of jail and out of a gang. "You're the best man I've ever known, Tim Means. I just wish we had more time."

She didn't even ask him to come with her because she knew—he couldn't leave this place or their people. Tim was as much a part of the White Sandy as the sun in the sky.

He stared at her with such longing it took her breath away. "So do I, babe."

And she couldn't even hold him right now because Georgey was between them, bleeding and wounded and her heart was breaking.

"Jesus, you two," Georgey croaked.

Summer startled, which made him moan. "You're awake!"

"Who can sleep with all this mushiness?" he mumbled. He was still ashen and his eyes were closed

203

tight, but she thought she saw a hint of smile on his lips. "Ever hear of long distance?"

Summer's head snapped up and her gaze collided with Tim's.

"Just saying. Buncha idiots…" Georgey's voice trailed off again and he relaxed in her arms.

Tim's eyes were wide and Summer had to believe hope brightened them a little. They began to speak over each other. "I could get a better internet connection and hire Ezra full-time…"

"We could come out when Georgey has an extra day off for school?"

"…Stay here for Christmas—I could go there for Thanksgiving?"

"Idiots," Georgey muttered. "Shoulda thought of that in the first place."

"Hush," Summer said. She wiped tears out of her eyes but these weren't tears of panic. "Could this work?"

"For you?" Tim reached over and with the back of his hand—thankfully blood-free—he stroked her cheek. "I'll make it work, Summer. Because home is wherever you are."

Epilogue

Four years later...

"Nervous?"

Summer sighed as Tim's arms encircled her waist, pulling her back against his chest. She never tired of the feel of his arms around her. God willing, she never would.

"Why would I be nervous? I'm not nervous. There's nothing to be nervous about," she said. Nervously.

"It's just a graduation party," Tim said, resting his chin on her shoulder. "You've been to graduation parties on the rez before."

She had. For the last four years, she'd spent her summers on the White Sandy, tutoring kids and watching Georgey relax in a way he never quite managed while living in Minneapolis.

"Correction—it's Georgey's graduation party. That's *huge*." It truly was. Considering Georgey had barely been able to read when she'd become part of his life, graduating from high school was a major accomplishment. Yes, he was almost twenty-one, but he'd made it through by sheer force of will.

And a lot of nagging from Summer. She wanted this moment to be perfect for him. In all honesty, she kind of wanted it to be perfect for herself. She wasn't a part-time Indian anymore and, at least in her mind, this party marked the start of her living on the White Sandy—and with Tim Means—full time.

Which was a lot to ask of any one party, frankly. "I mean, his mom is coming, for heaven's sake."

Tim chuckled in her ear. God, she never got tired of the sound. "You've met Eileen before, babe."

Summer turned her head to give the man she loved A Look. "Was that supposed to make me feel better? Because it's not working."

Not considering the last time Eileen Crow Dog had bothered to put in an appearance—at her own mother's funeral two years ago—Tim had been forced to call in Ezra Johnson, his deputy, to arrest the woman.

At least Tim hadn't arrested her himself. Score one for family harmony.

Still, Summer had agreed to include Eileen today for one simple reason. "It's important to Georgey that she's here. So she'll be here." He might never see his mother again and she wanted him to have one more good memory of the woman who'd tried to raise him. Even if she hadn't succeeded.

"She'll be on her best behavior." Tim didn't say *or else* but Summer heard it anyway.

She smiled to herself. Tim loved Georgey like…well, maybe not like a son. But like a brother, definitely. She and Tim both walked that line between sibling and parent. But at least they walked it together. That was the important part. "I'm glad I'm here," she said, holding him tight.

"I'm glad you're here, too. There's no place else I'd want you to be."

Was it her imagination or did Sheriff Tim Means sound nervous, too?

Surely not. The man wasn't capable of anxiety. For four long years, he'd been her rock of stability as she'd shepherded Georgey into adulthood. Long video calls, longer drives, intense weekends together—through it all, Tim Means was unflappable.

No, she was just projecting her own anxiety onto him. She looked out across the community room she'd reserved for the party at Sinte Gliske Community College, checking to see if there was anything she'd missed. This was the first party she'd thrown herself and she wanted it to be just *right*.

Everything looked perfect. Two banners hung over a long table set with punch, snacks and five huge cakes decorated with enough icing to put the entire tribe into diabetic shock. One read, "Congrats H.S. Grad!" and the other, "GO ARMY."

A table by the doorway was laden with store-bought blankets, towels and pillows, as well as baby blankets, hats, scarves and mittens Summer had started knitting for just this occasion four long years ago. Giveaways were an important part of any celebratory milestone out on the rez and she wanted to put her own touch on it.

Then Georgey walked into the room, his military dress clothes highlighting just how damn much he'd grown over the years. Summer's breath caught at the sight of him. She hadn't seen him in almost three months—Tim had been the one to pick Georgey up at the airport and drive him home to the rez. Since then, he'd kept out of sight.

Now she knew why. She wasn't going to get

through this without crying. "Oh, Georgey," she said, blinking back the tears. "You look like... "

"A warrior," Tim finished for her, pride in his voice. "Your dad would be proud, son."

Georgey gave them a salute and Summer couldn't take it anymore. She threw her arms around his chest and hugged her little brother.

Who was, of course, about eight inches taller than she was. He'd grown into his hands and feet and broadened both with regular meals and basic training.

One thing was clear—he was not her *little* brother. Not anymore.

"I'm so proud of you," she said, her voice cracking. Maybe they should have had this little reunion in private, not right before the big event, so she could cry her happy tears and not worry about smudging her makeup.

"Geez, sis—don't do that. It's embarrassing," he said, but he couldn't even pull petulant off anymore. His voice was too deep and his eyes shone bright with unshed tears. Before she could scold him, he pulled her back into a fierce hug. "Missed you, Summer."

"I missed you, too, Georgey. Sort of," she added, just because she could. They laughed and that helped with the tears.

Living with Georgey for four years had been a challenge, even on the good days. She hadn't been able to afford a bigger place and it hadn't taken them long to learn each other's irritating quirks.

But for all that, she'd loved having her brother with her. Her mother Linda had basically stopped speaking to her and, if Summer hadn't had Georgey to focus on and Tim waiting for her, she might have crumbled in the face of such rejection.

But she'd had Georgey and Tim and, when she could make the trip out to the White Sandy, the rest of the tribe. Well, that part was at an end. She wasn't going to spend another second making long-distance video calls or counting the days until the next weekend one of them could make the long drive.

Four long years of focusing on Georgey first were finally at an end. He'd flown through basic training with flying colors, thanks to Tim doing his best to prepare Georgey for military life. He was heading out for his first tour in a few days and then...

This was her home now. *Tim* was her home. True, he hadn't asked her to marry him yet, but hell, that was just a piece of paper. She'd happily live in sin for the rest of her life if that's what Tim wanted.

People began to trickle in—kids Georgey had gone to school with, families of littler kids he'd played soccer with at the Child Care Center, veterans who always, *always* turned out to honor another warrior. The whole tribe showed up, it seemed.

Shorty came with his younger sister and his mother. After Levi had been sent to prison, Shorty had come back to the rez, finished high school and had just completed his first year at Sinte Gliske. He had a job working cattle for Jacob Plenty Holes on the far side of the rez. Summer couldn't be prouder of the kid.

Jeremy, the kid Georgey had saved at the pow wow, came with his entire family, which meant Georgey got hugged *again*. As far as Summer could tell, Jeremy's mom cried and hugged Georgey every single time she saw him. Georgey shot Summer a desperate look as the woman clung to him, but all Summer did was laugh.

209

Circle came back from college at South Dakota State, where she'd gotten a scholarship after earning her GED. She spent her summers at the Child Care Center and had plans to become a special education teacher. Although no one said anything about it, Summer got the feeling she was waiting for Georgey. But was Georgey waiting for Circle? Summer didn't know. He'd dated in Minneapolis, but nothing serious. Not like the way Circle walked up to him, her eyes wide, and certainly not like how Georgey pulled her into his arms and kissed her hard.

People kept coming. Rebel Runs Fast and Dr. Madeline Mitchell showed up with their daughter Kathleen who, at three, just sat in her father's arms and watched the whole party with huge, soulful eyes while Madeline caught up with some of the older guests. Summer figured that, with Rebel and Madeline as parents, Kathleen was going to grow up to run the world.

Clarence and Tammy Thunder arrived next with their kids in tow—Mikey, now a cocky ten-year-old with a mind that still moved a mile a minute and Farrah, who announced to anyone sitting down that she was four and a half, going on five. Farrah was followed by Katie, who was just starting to walk, much to Flo Tall Tree's delight. Then, tucked against one of Clarence's shoulders was little Sean who, at three months old, was starting to smile at everyone and everything.

Nobody and Melonie Bodine showed up, which made Summer smile. Jamie Bodine, now sixteen, gravitated to Georgey and within seconds, the two guys were deep in conversation while Circle sat on the ground, singing to the babies. Jamie might very well wind up in the military. Heaven knew the boy had been raised with a strict code of honor. The Bodine girls, as twins Susanna and Sophia were known because they were identical and no one—except for Nobody and, on good days, Melonie—could tell them apart, made straight for their cousin Kathleen. Within seconds, the trio of three-year-olds were in danger of upending the table of cake. Melonie got there first and saved the table while Nobody swooped up his daughters, smiling as they shrieked with glee.

Summer let the laughter and chatter wash over her. The men congregated around the punch and talked of old battles and old loves, as well as new ones. The women were by the cakes, keeping a close eye on the kids and talking about birthdays and anniversaries. The grandparents took over the chairs, laughing and singing and enjoying the heck out of having Georgey serve them cake in his dress clothes.

Eileen Crow Dog showed up late. She looked terrible—a lifetime of alcohol abuse was catching up to her, but at least she seemed sober today. Summer watched from a safe distance as Eileen hugged her son and patted his arm and even smiled at him. It was, hands down, the most maternal Summer had ever seen the woman act and Georgey beamed down at her.

There. Georgey had his moment. The party, as far as Summer was concerned, was a total success.

She sighed with happiness. This was what she'd missed growing up, but she wasn't going to miss out on it ever again. These were her people but more than that, they were her family. They always had been, even when she hadn't known it. Summer loved them all.

She'd resigned at the end of the last school year and left her apartment in Minneapolis behind. She'd officially moved in with Tim and, even though the front door still stuck, she loved actually living with the man. They cooked dinner together and turned everything they could into a date, even if it was just a grocery run. And when the weather was right, they headed out for the middle of nowhere and made love on the hood of the car.

It was perfect. Even if it meant that Georgey still had to sleep on the couch when he was home on leave.

Even now, she glanced back at where Tim was laughing—actually laughing—at something Nobody Bodine had said. She loved being here, loved having this celebration with her whole family. But she'd be lying if she said she wasn't looking forward to later tonight, when Georgey went out with his friends and she had Tim all to herself for a few hours.

The years had barely touched the man. Aside from a streak of white coming in at his temples—which he blamed entirely on either Georgey or Nobody, depending on the day—Tim was as rock-solid and gorgeous as he'd been the day he'd found Summer lost on the White Sandy. The first day she'd come home.

She might have loved him from the beginning. Her summer fling had become so much *more.*

And now she'd moved out here to be with him. She even had a job. Technically, two jobs. She continued to tutor students for their GEDs at Sinte Gliske every weekday morning and she'd began to contact the area high school teachers about student retention and college preparation classes. Which was nice because she didn't have to teach Shakespeare anymore.

The Mitchell Foundation, a trust run by Dr. Madeline Mitchell and Melonie Bodine, was funding the construction of a new after-school center next to the Child Care Center. The Teen Reach Center would be geared for kids ages twelve and up and, in addition to having plentiful snacks and homework help, the foundation was also footing the bill for an outdoor skate park and basketball courts, as well as computers and books. Lots of books, graphic novels and audio books. There wasn't a library outside of a school on the reservation, so Summer was dedicating one whole wall to young adult literature.

The kids on the White Sandy needed a place to go where they could be warm in the winter and get a meal they might not get at home. Teen Reach would be a place where they could still be kids, get homework help and, most importantly, stay connected to the tribe without joining a gang or falling through the cracks, like Georgey almost had.

Summer was in charge of the whole thing. It was terrifying and wonderful at the same time, because this was how she fit into Tim's world. She might not have the skills to change diapers but she could be here for kids navigating puberty and adulthood and, hopefully, keep them out of Tim's jail.

She was chatting with Melonie Bodine about how they were going to decorate the skate park—decorating was Melonie's strong suit—when she caught Tim and Georgey with their heads together, both glancing at her over their shoulders.

She knew that look. Those two were up to something. She turned, but Madeline appeared next to her. "How's it going?" she asked in that tone of voice that made it clear she expected—nay, *demanded*—an answer. Summer liked Madeline Mitchell a great deal, but the woman had a way about her that could be off-putting, to say the least.

"Fine," Summer said suspiciously.

Madeline and Melonie shared a look, then Tammy Thunder was with them, also staring at Summer while she tried and largely failed not to smile. "How's it going?"

"Fine," Summer repeated. "What's going on?"

"Nothing!" All three women said at once in too-loud voices.

"Uh huh." Summer narrowed her eyes at them, but their collective smiles held. "Then what's going on behind me?"

"Nothing!" they all but shouted in unison.

So that was a *something*. "Is it bad? One of the kids tip over the punch bowl?" Or worse, was Eileen making a scene?

"No," Tammy said, giving up the fight against that smile. "If there *were* something going on behind you—"

"Which there isn't," Melonie cut in.

"It'd be a good thing," Madeline finished.

They all smiled again. Even bigger this time.

No, that wasn't suspicious at all.

"Summer?" The sound of Tim's voice cut through the room, sending a shiver of want down her back. The room went silent in a heartbeat. Or maybe that was just her pulse pounding in her veins, drowning out all other noise.

Something was definitely going on. What was that man doing?

"You can look now," Melonie whispered with a wink.

She turned slowly and found Tim standing in the middle of the room, a bouquet of roses in his hand and a smile on his face. Behind him, a circle of their friends and family stood, all looking hopeful and expectant. Georgey was at his shoulder, grinning wildly. "What... "

But that was as far as she got before Tim fell to one knee. She gasped, her hands flying to her chest as the women behind her pushed her forward.

"I never thought I'd meet a woman like you," Tim began, his voice low and serious and, yes, nervous. "I love this land and I love my people—my family."

The crowd behind him made a happy humming noise because, no matter what, they loved him, too.

Oh, God—this was really happening. Tim was down on bended knee and he was proposing. To her! In front of everyone! At Georgey's party!

"But," Tim went on, "being the sheriff has meant that, too often, it's a tough love and it makes it hard for anyone to love me back. Before you came to the rez, I'd resigned myself to a life on the edge and it was a damned lonely place to be. Then Georgey happened and—"

"Hey!" Georgey protested, but he did it with a smile.

"You came for him and the moment I saw you, lost in the middle of nowhere." Everyone chuckled at that, even Summer. "I saw someone more. Someone who didn't look at me and see just a lawman. Instead, you saw a man and I loved you for it."

"Oh, Tim," she tried to say, but her throat closed and she had trouble getting the words out.

He held out his hand for her and she walked forward. Or maybe she was pushed again. In his palm was a simple ring with a small, round diamond set in rose gold. "We've spent too much time apart," he went on. "And I don't ever want to be apart from you again. You are my past, my present and I want you to be my future." He took a deep breath and said, "Summer Collins, would you marry me?"

"Preferably before I ship out," Georgey added. "I wouldn't want to miss my favorite sister getting hitched."

Circle, bless her heart, smacked Georgey on the arm and shushed him.

Tim rolled his eyes, which made Summer laugh.

"We're already living together," she reminded him. Instantly, alarm widened his eyes. The room felt like it was holding its breath. "But I want something more from you, Tim Means. I want it all. I want you as my family. Because we are all family."

Tim almost sagged with relief.

Summer knew she was crying but she was powerless to stop. "Yes," she told him, holding out her hand to him. "I'll be a wife to your husband. There's nothing I want more."

"Thank God," he said, slipping the ring onto her finger. He pushed himself to his feet and, thrusting the roses back for Georgey to hold, folded her into his arms. "I'm yours," he whispered against her lips. "Stay with me, for the rest of our lives."

"I will, because I'm yours, too," she whispered back. Then he was kissing her and she was kissing him back in front of everyone and people were hooting and clapping and when she and Tim broke apart, there were handshakes and hugs and plans to be made.

She was home because she was with Tim.

Forever.

Thank you so much for reading *The Sheriff*! I hope you enjoyed it!

Would you like to know when my next book is available? You can sign up for my new release email alerts at www.sarahmanderson.com.

I appreciate all reviews, both positive and negative, because reviews help other readers find books they'll enjoy. If you would like to leave a review, you can do so on the vendor at which you purchased this book and/or on Goodreads.

The Sheriff is the fifth book in the Men of the White Sandy series. Other titles in the series are *The Medicine Man* (Book 1), *The Rancher* (Book 2), *The Shadow* (Book 3), and *The Medic* (Book 4).

About the Author

Award-winning author Sarah M. Anderson may live east of the Mississippi River, but her heart lies out west on the Great Plains. When she started writing, it wasn't long before her characters found themselves out in South Dakota among the Lakota Sioux. She loves to put people from two different worlds into new situations and see how their backgrounds and cultures take them someplace they never thought they'd go.

With over 1.2 million copies published in over twenty-one countries, Sarah has published over 40 books. Sarah's book *A Man of Privilege* won a RT Book Reviews 2012 Reviewers' Choice Best Book Award. *The Nanny Plan* was a 2016 RITA® winner for Best Contemporary: Short. Additionally, Sarah has given workshops at national and regional conferences, taught craft classes online, spoken at libraries and book clubs, and published articles in the Romance Writers Report. Find out more about Sarah's books at www.sarahmanderson.com. and sign up for the new-release newsletter at http://eepurl.com/nv39b.

Readers can find out more about Sarah's love of cowboys and Indians at:

Her Newsletter: http://eepurl.com/nv39b

Her Website: www.sarahmanderson.com

On Facebook: www.facebook.com/pages/Sarah-M-Anderson-Author

On Twitter: @SarahMAnderson1

On Goodreads:
www.goodreads.com/author/show/4982413.Sarah_M_Anderson

By Snail Mail at: Sarah M. Anderson, 200 N 8th ST #193, Quincy IL 62301-9996

Other Books by Sarah M. Anderson

Men of the White Sandy
The Medicine Man
The Rancher
The Shadow
The Medic
The Sheriff
The Wannabe Cowboy

Lawyers in Love
A Man of His Word
A Man of Privilege
A Man of Distinction
Pride and Pregnancy

The Boltons
Straddling the Line
Bringing Home the Bachelor
Expecting a Bolton Baby
Little Secrets: Claiming His Pregnant Bride

Rich, Rugged Ranchers
A Real Cowboy

The Texas Cattleman's Club
What a Rancher Wants
His Lost and Found Family
A Surprise for the Sheikh

Dynasties: The Newports
Claimed by the Cowboy

Rodeo Dreamers
Rodeo Dreams
One Rodeo Season
Crushing on the Cowboy

The First Family of Rodeo
His Best Friend's Sister
His Enemy's Daughter
His for One Night

The Beaumont Heirs
Not the Boss's Baby
Seduced by the Cowboy
A Beaumont Christmas Wedding
His Son, Her Secret
Falling for Her Fake Fiancé
His Illegitimate Heir
Rich Rancher for Christmas
Billionaire's Baby Promise

Billionaires and Babies
The Nanny Plan
His Forever Family
Twins for the Billionaire
Seduction on His Terms

Holiday Novellas
The Christmas Pony

NotMyFirstRodeo.com
Something About a Cowboy
Roping a Rancher

Writing as Maggie Chase

The Jeweled Ladies: The Mistress Series
His Topaz
Their Emerald
Her Ebony
His Sapphire
His Crown Jewel

The Jeweled Ladies: The Rogues Series
His Diamond
Their Amethyst

The Wannabe Cowboy

© 2019 by Sarah M. Anderson

Next to the White Sandy is the Last Chance Ranch…

Zack Baker is down to his last chance and the only person who can help him is Samantha Kenady, owner of the L/C Ranch. He's hoping to use his good looks and charm to convince her to let him finish the zoological study he needs to complete his Ph.D. He needs to get the permission of Ms. Kenady because her land is one of the few places where the foxes he's studying live. He'll do whatever it takes to finish his thesis.

Things get off to a rocky start when he has a run-in with a cowboy—except it's not a cowboy. It's a cowgirl—Sam. Scarred by an attack that happened when she was a teenager, Sam finds a measure of redemption in taking in cast-offs and strays. She may not be able to erase her own past, but she can help others start over. Sam runs her ranch with an iron hand. Her rules are nonnegotiable, and rule #1 is no men.

But some rules can be bent—and others can be broken. Does Sam dare risk it all on a wannabe cowboy, or will their attraction cause everything she's worked so hard to protect to go up in smoke?

Excerpt from The Wannabe Cowboy

A nd A man came out of the tent wearing nothing but a pair of boxers. Plaid, she guessed. He stood up and stretched in the early morning light. His bare chest was right at eye level.

Whoa. Maybe she did need to get out more, because the prospect of a mostly naked man was making her a little lightheaded. It's not that she didn't see shirtless men—Heaven kept her all up-to-date on what the latest Hollywood hunks were doing—but this was different. When she saw a hot dude shirtless on the TV, she didn't think much of it. Now, here, face to face with a real man's real chest, she felt... funny.

Aware.

She blinked against the brightening light, but the image didn't change. Broad shoulders led to long arms. His chest was smooth but he had more than enough muscles. The sight of that chest made her own tighten. The legs weren't bad, either. Not scrawny chicken legs, but not the tree trunks that came on some of the local cowboys. No, he was well-proportioned. Good looking. He was—

Shucking his shorts.

Her mouth dropped open at the sight before her. *Whoa.*

Good morning, sunshine, was all she could think. Then the guy pivoted. Hell.

Sam flattened herself against the ground. What would he do if he caught her watching? She had no idea what kind of man was squatting on her land. Not a Gunderson, that much she was pretty sure about. Gundersons didn't make her feel all funny, shorts or no shorts. But that left the field wide open between tree-hugger and psychopath.

She hugged her rifle, waiting. Agonizingly long seconds passed as she wondered whether or not a naked man was about to jump her.

The grass was quiet, but the water started talking to her. She heard the splash of the creek. He was swimming?

She leaned up. He was swimming, all right. She could just see a curved set of cheeks disappear in *her* creek. He ducked his head under the water and then began to... shampoo? Really?

He was taking a bath at, what? Six in morning? That creek couldn't be much above sixty-five degrees. She was staring. But he was naked in her water. Staring seemed like an even trade-off.

His back matched his front, strong without being muscle-bound. And she'd already gotten a good look at everything else. A well-built man, no doubt about it.

He started out of the water, and she couldn't help but look. How cold had that water been?

Cold. But he was still impressive.

She shook her head. She was staring at a naked man, and she hadn't even had her coffee yet.

He wrapped a towel around his waist, shook the water from his hair, and lifted his face to the sun.

She gaped in silent shock.

225

Baker. Zack Baker was naked. In her creek. On her land.

Was she seriously crouched in the grass, getting kind of hot for the fox guy? The one who hadn't even realized she was a woman?

He may not have figured she was a female, but damned if Sam wasn't aware of him as a man. And it wasn't just because she'd gotten a full look at him. It'd been a long time since anyone had made her stare.

Nope. She was not going to stare at him as he dried off. She was absolutely not going to get the hots for him.

Except she was, damn it, and that shouldn't happen. She was the boss around here. She did what had to be done. Which was not gawking at a hot guy skinny-dipping. She had to get this guy off her land. It didn't matter how hot—or naked—he was.

Baker slipped his shorts back on, checked the coffee and disappeared back into the tent.

Unbelievable.

She put the safety on the rifle and crept down the hill. She could hear him rattling around in his tent. *At least he kept a neat site*, she thought as she crouched down in front of the fire. The fire was in a pit lined with river stones and the coffee perking away on a grate. He'd hung his food in a bear bag on one of the pines near the water. She couldn't smell the latrine and she didn't see any garbage, just a clothesline strung between the tent and the tree.

He'd been here a while—long enough to do laundry.

Freaking unbelievable.

He was humming what sounded like "Rocky Mountain High." Sitting on her heels, she kept the rifle on her lap and poured herself a cup of coffee. Tasted like brown water. Good. She needed to stay focused.

Zack Baker came out of the tent, t-shirt in hand, jeans up but not buttoned, still humming.

Awareness hit her again. When was the last time she'd been this close to a half-dressed man with a good chest? The better question was, when was the last time she'd wanted to be this close to a half-dressed man?

He hadn't seen her yet. She almost smiled as she said, "You make lousy coffee."

At the sound of her voice, he froze, one arm in a sleeve. Sam let her eyes take in all of that chest. Good? Hell, it bordered on amazing. Wasn't her fault it was just about at eye level.

A moment of stillness followed while she waited for him to make his play. She took another sip of the coffee. At least it was hot.

He seemed to notice she was staring. His gaze caught hers and dragged it up to his face. One eyebrow notched up while half of that charming grin she'd seen two weeks ago took up residence on his face. Moving real slow, he pulled the shirt over his head and found her eyes again as he ran his fingers through his hair. Finally, he spoke. "I didn't hear you get here."

"I expect not, what with all the humming." She managed to break his gaze, but found herself staring at his open fly. Plaid boxers, red and blue. They matched his reddish curls pretty well. "You want to button up there?"

She should not be staring as a man—a stranger— closed a five-button fly with one hand, but she couldn't help it. Baker's fingers worked with a speed that was both nimble and surprising. If Heaven were here, Sam knew she'd make some comment about how

227

he was good with his hands. But Heaven wasn't here and Sam kept her thoughts to herself.

When he was done, she looked up and saw the full-on smolder. That smolder seemed to say "good with my hands" and a whole hell of a lot more.

"I suppose you're wondering what I'm doing here."

Interesting. Whereas his eyes were all confidence, his voice sounded more like he knew exactly how shaky his position was.

If he had his shirt on, she didn't feel like she was peeping. Right? "As a matter of fact, I am, being as I'm certain I told you to leave."

He swallowed again, his eyes cutting down to the rifle in her lap. "You did."

"And yet here we are."

www.ingramcontent.com/pod-product-compliance
Lightning Source LLC
Chambersburg PA
CBHW060429180626
46817CB00007B/2726